ZIG AND WIKKI

IN

SOMETHING ATE MY HOMEWORK

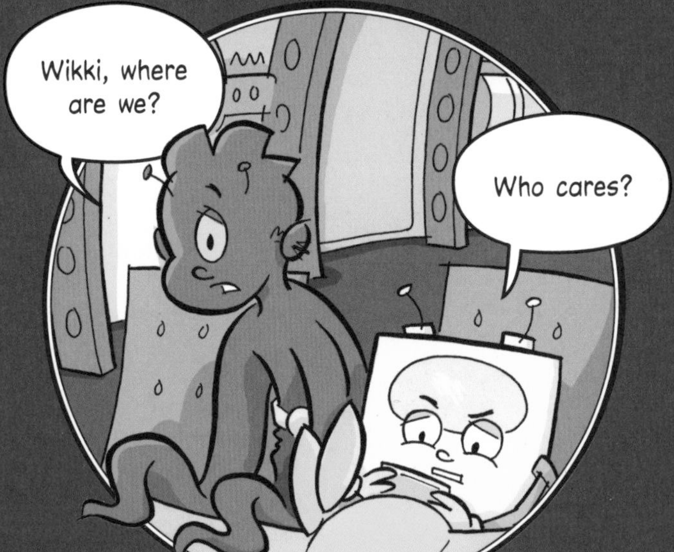
Wikki, where are we?
Who cares?

A TOON BOOK BY

NADJA SPIEGELMAN & TRADE LOEFFLER

AN IMPRINT OF CANDLEWICK PRESS

For my mother

–Nadja

For Mohammad Riza

–Trade

Editorial Director: FRANÇOISE MOULY
Advisor: ART SPIEGELMAN

Book Design: FRANÇOISE MOULY & JONATHAN BENNETT

Guest Editor: GEOFFREY HAYES
Guest Nature Researcher: JUDY FUNK

All photos used by permission, all rights reserved. Page 13: © Mailthepic / Dreamstime.com; Page 14: © 2008 Terrence Jacobs; Page 18: © Le Do / Dreamstime.com; Page 21: © Clearviewstock / Dreamstime.com; Page 22: © 2007 Maianna Fitzgerald; Page 30: © 2009 Lyn Chesna; Page 40: Fly larva © 2009 Luis Buján, Dragonfly © Tanya Puntti (tanya-ann.com), Frog © Alptraum / Dreamstime.com, Raccoon © Eric Isselée / Dreamstime.com. BACKCOVER: Frog © Shao Weiwei / Dreamstime.com.
The Library of Congress has cataloged the hardcover edition as follows:
Spiegelman, Nadja.
Zig and Wikki in something ate my homework / a TOON book by Nadja Spiegelman & Trade Loeffler.
p. cm.   Summary: Zig and Wikki arrive on earth to seach for a pet for Zig's class assignment.   1. Graphic novels. [1. Graphic novels. 2. Pets–Fiction. 3. Science fiction.] I. Loeffler, Trade, ill. II. Title.
PZ7.7.S65Zi 2010   [Fic]–dc22   2009028017   ISBN 978-1-935179-02-3 (hardcover)
ISBN: 978-1-935179-38-2 (paperback)

13 14 15 16 17 18 TWP 10 9 8 7 6 5 4 3 2 1

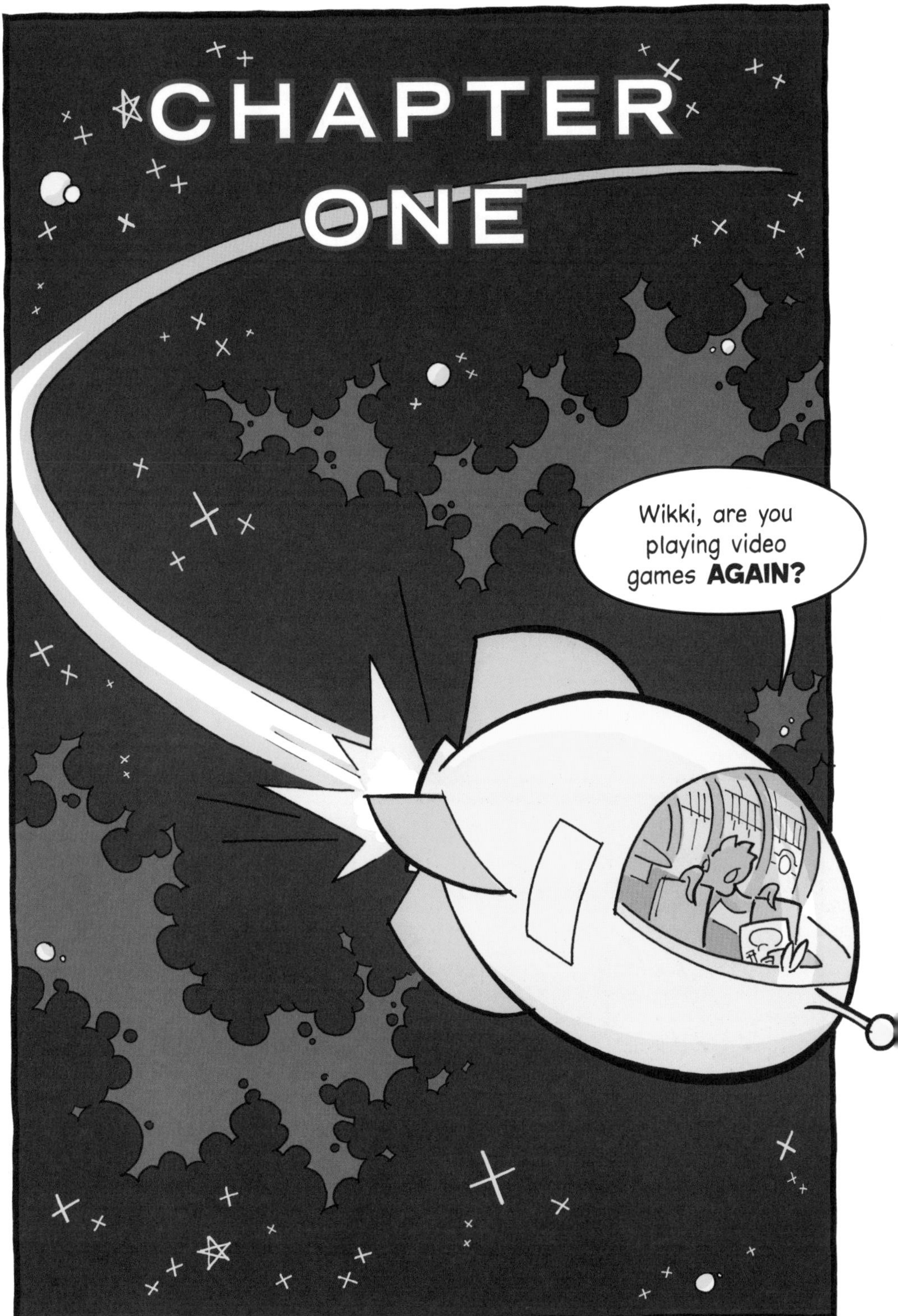
CHAPTER ONE
Wikki, are you playing video games AGAIN?

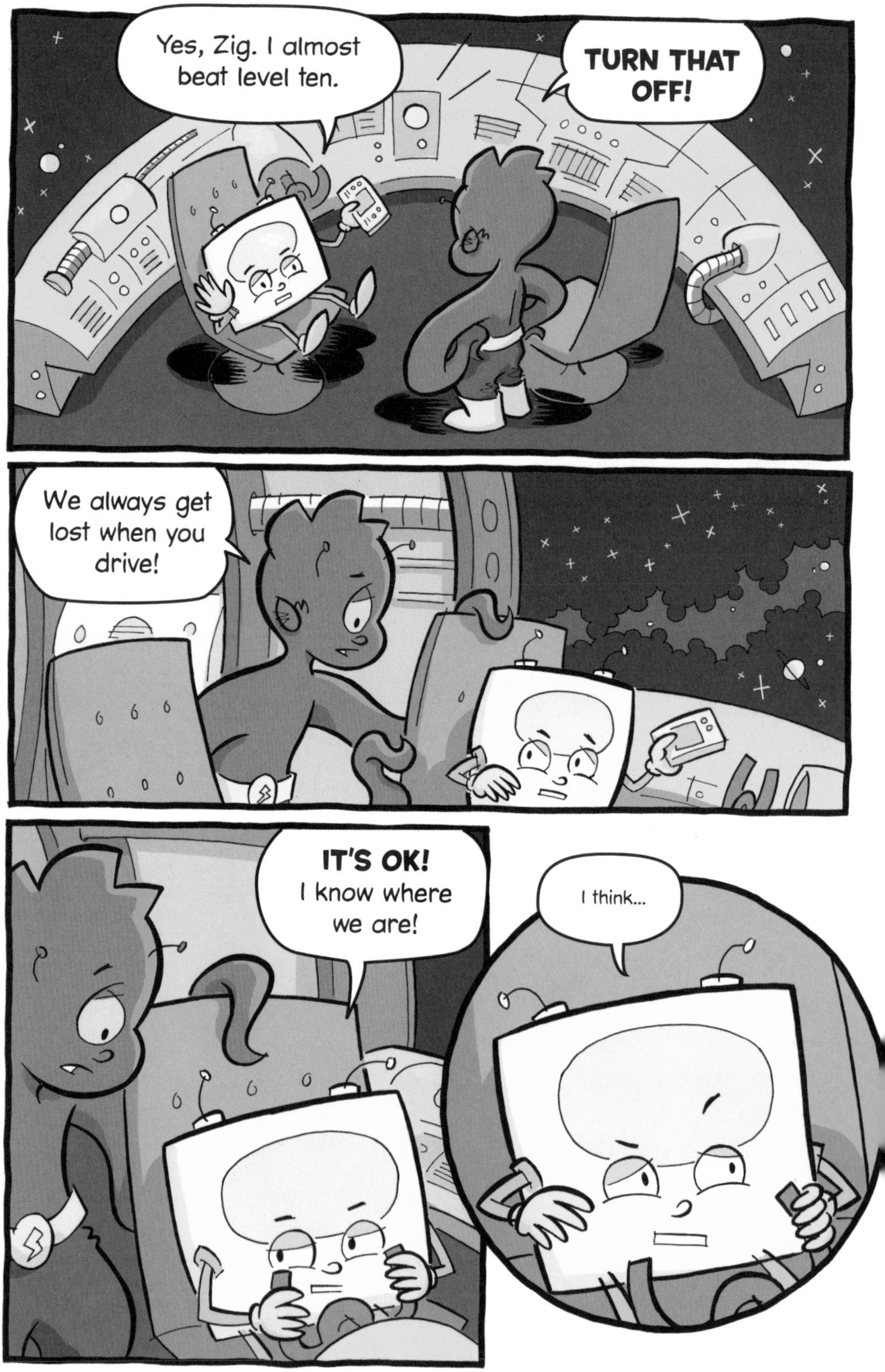
Yes, Zig. I almost beat level ten.
TURN THAT OFF!
We always get lost when you drive!
IT'S OK! I know where we are!
I think...

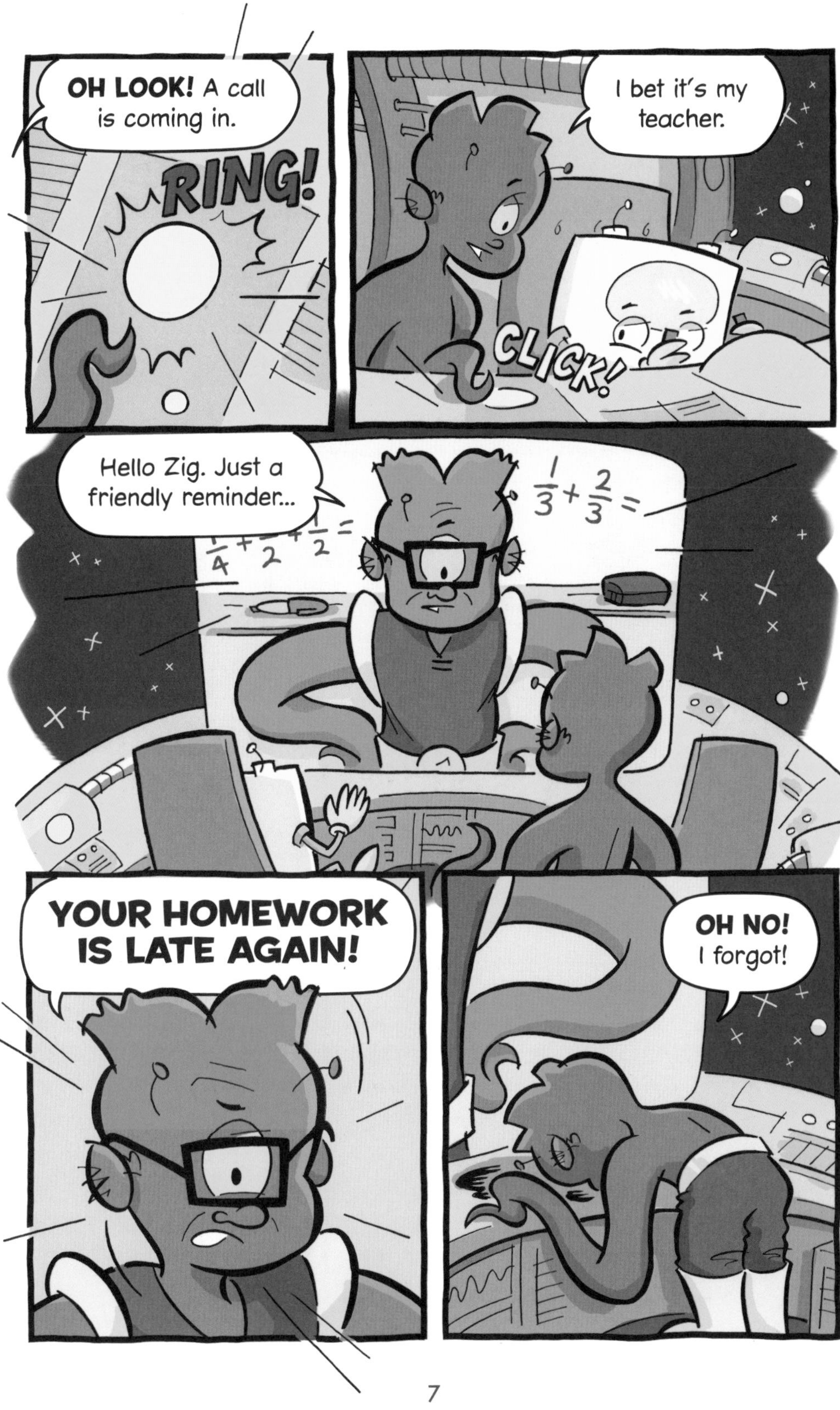
OH LOOK! A call is coming in.
RING!
I bet it's my teacher.
CLICK!
Hello Zig. Just a friendly reminder...
YOUR HOMEWORK IS LATE AGAIN!
OH NO! I forgot!

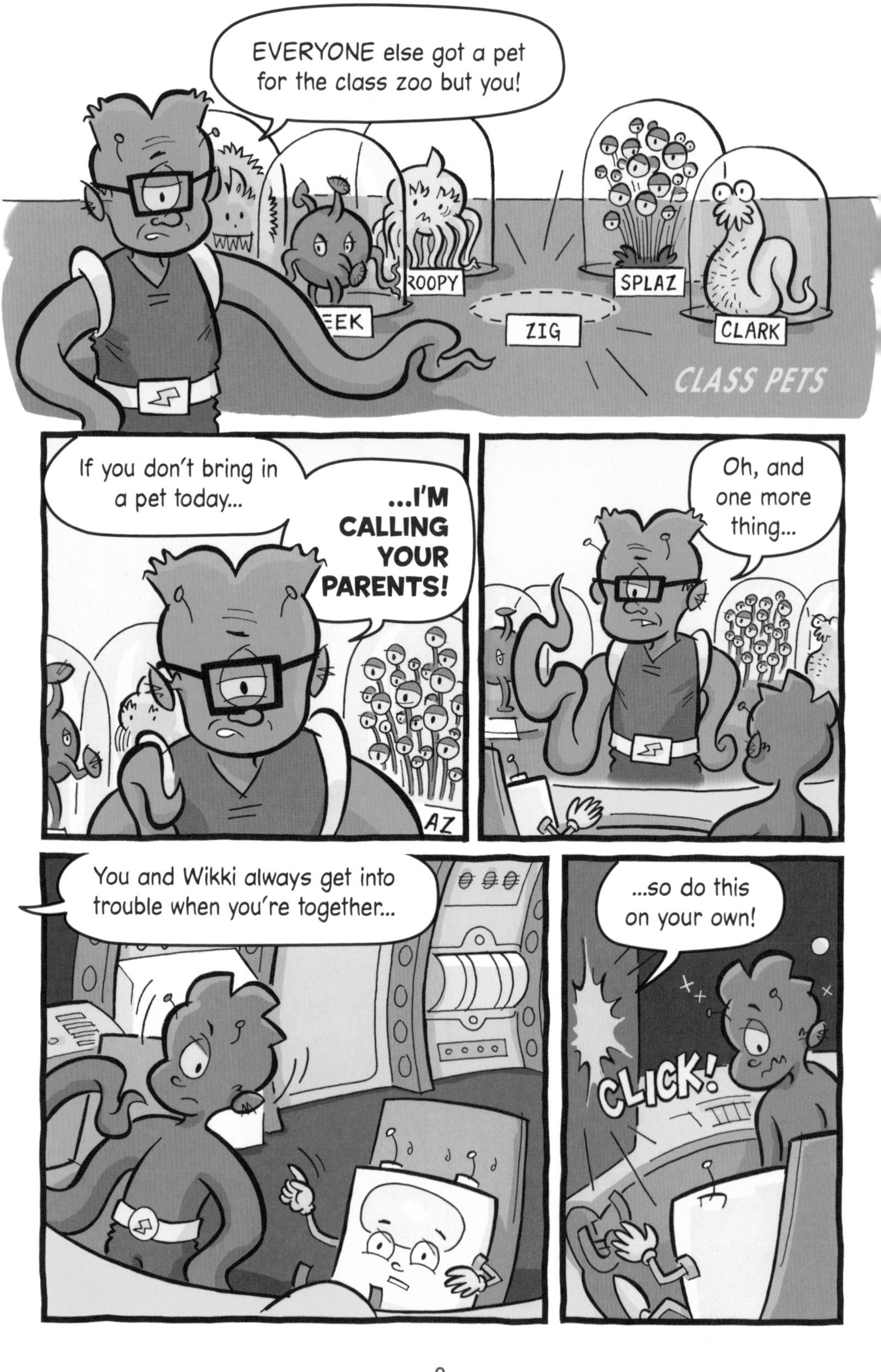
EVERYONE else got a pet for the class zoo but you!
ROOPY
EEK
ZIG
SPLAZ
CLARK
CLASS PETS
If you don't bring in a pet today...
...I'M CALLING YOUR PARENTS!
AZ
Oh, and one more thing...
You and Wikki always get into trouble when you're together...
...so do this on your own!
CLICK!

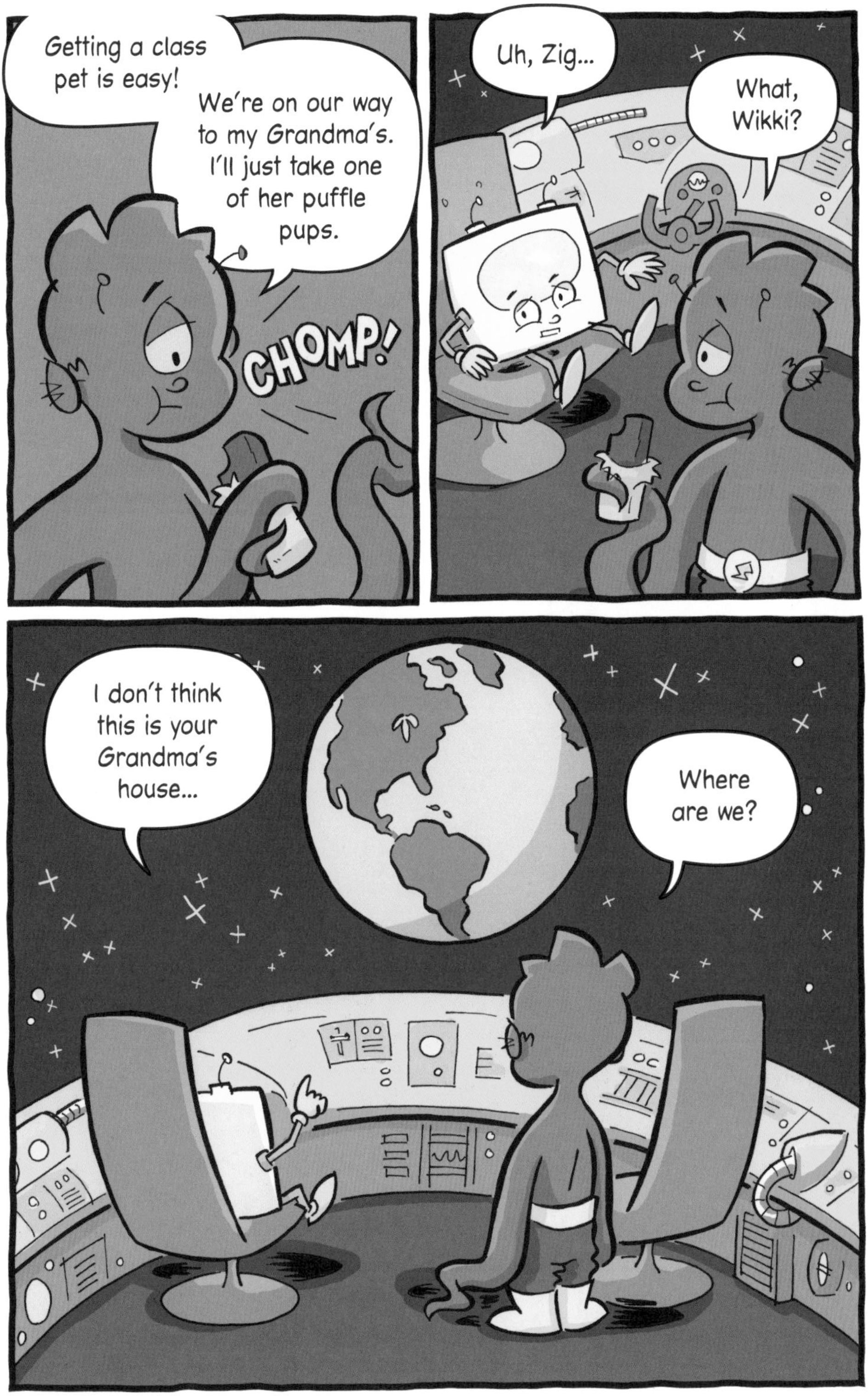
Getting a class pet is easy!
We're on our way to my Grandma's. I'll just take one of her puffle pups.
CHOMP!
Uh, Zig...
What, Wikki?
I don't think this is your Grandma's house...
Where are we?

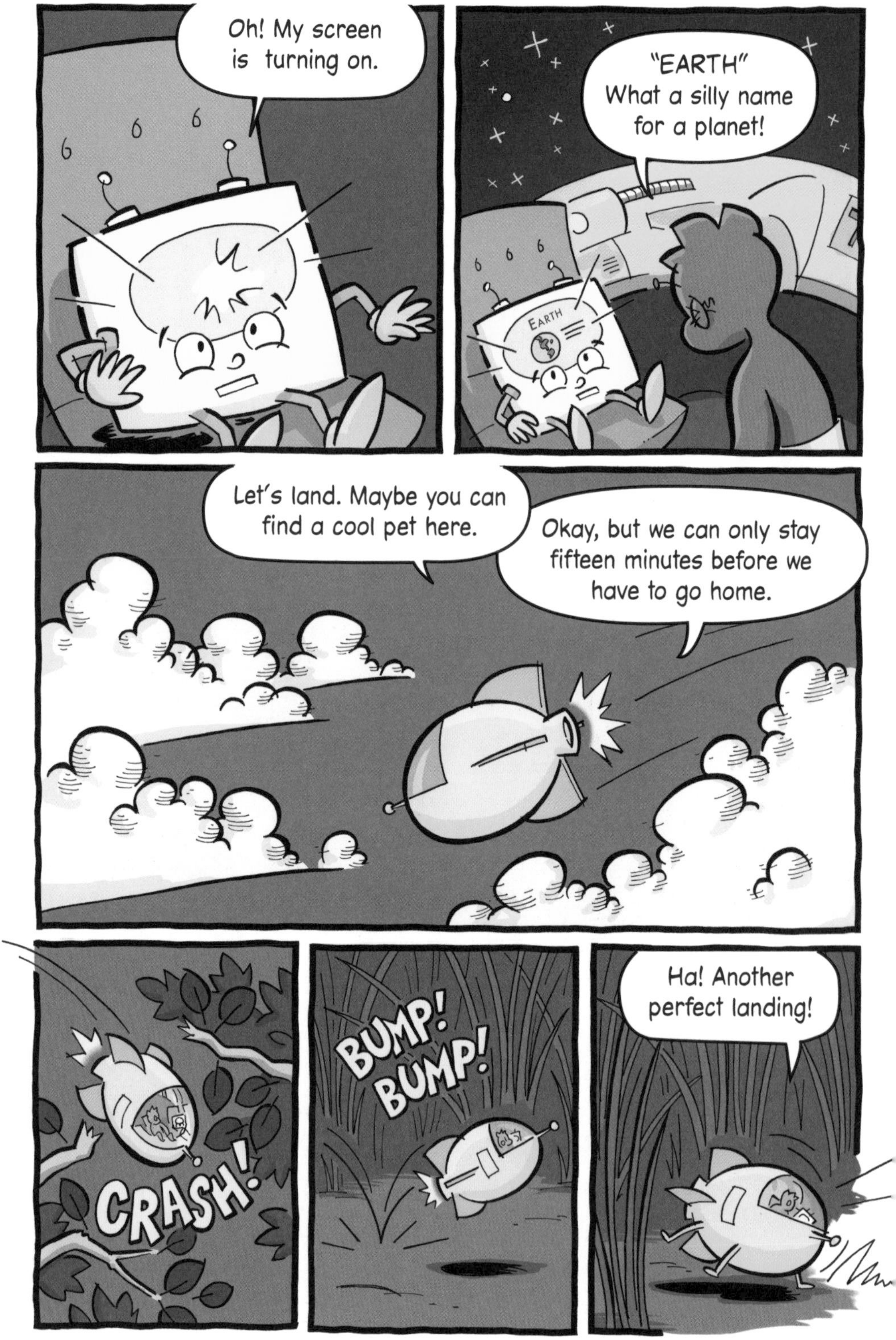
Oh! My screen is turning on.
EARTH
"EARTH" What a silly name for a planet!
Let's land. Maybe you can find a cool pet here.
Okay, but we can only stay fifteen minutes before we have to go home.
CRASH!
BUMP! BUMP!
Ha! Another perfect landing!

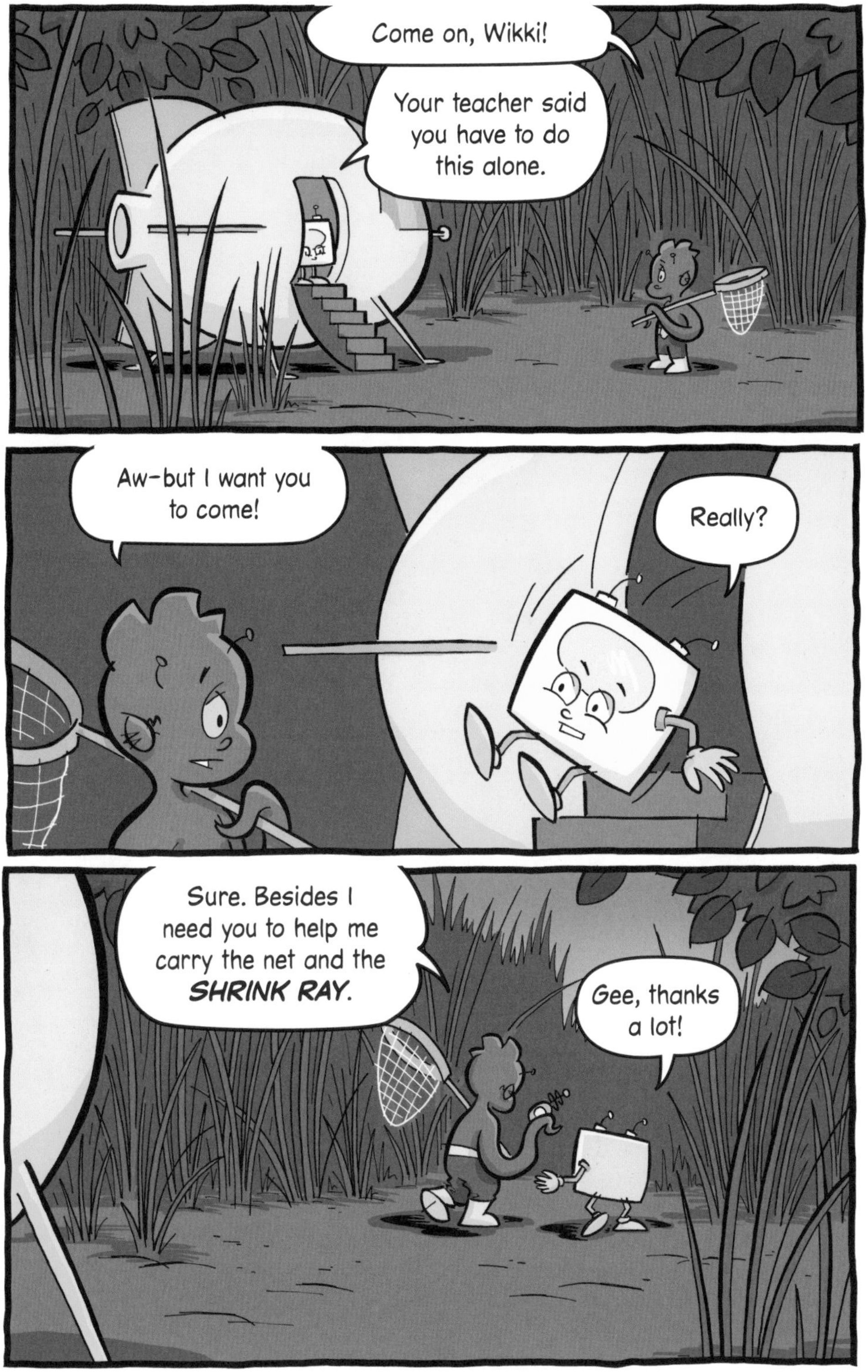
Come on, Wikki!
Your teacher said you have to do this alone.
Aw–but I want you to come!
Really?
Sure. Besides I need you to help me carry the net and the ***SHRINK RAY***.
Gee, thanks a lot!

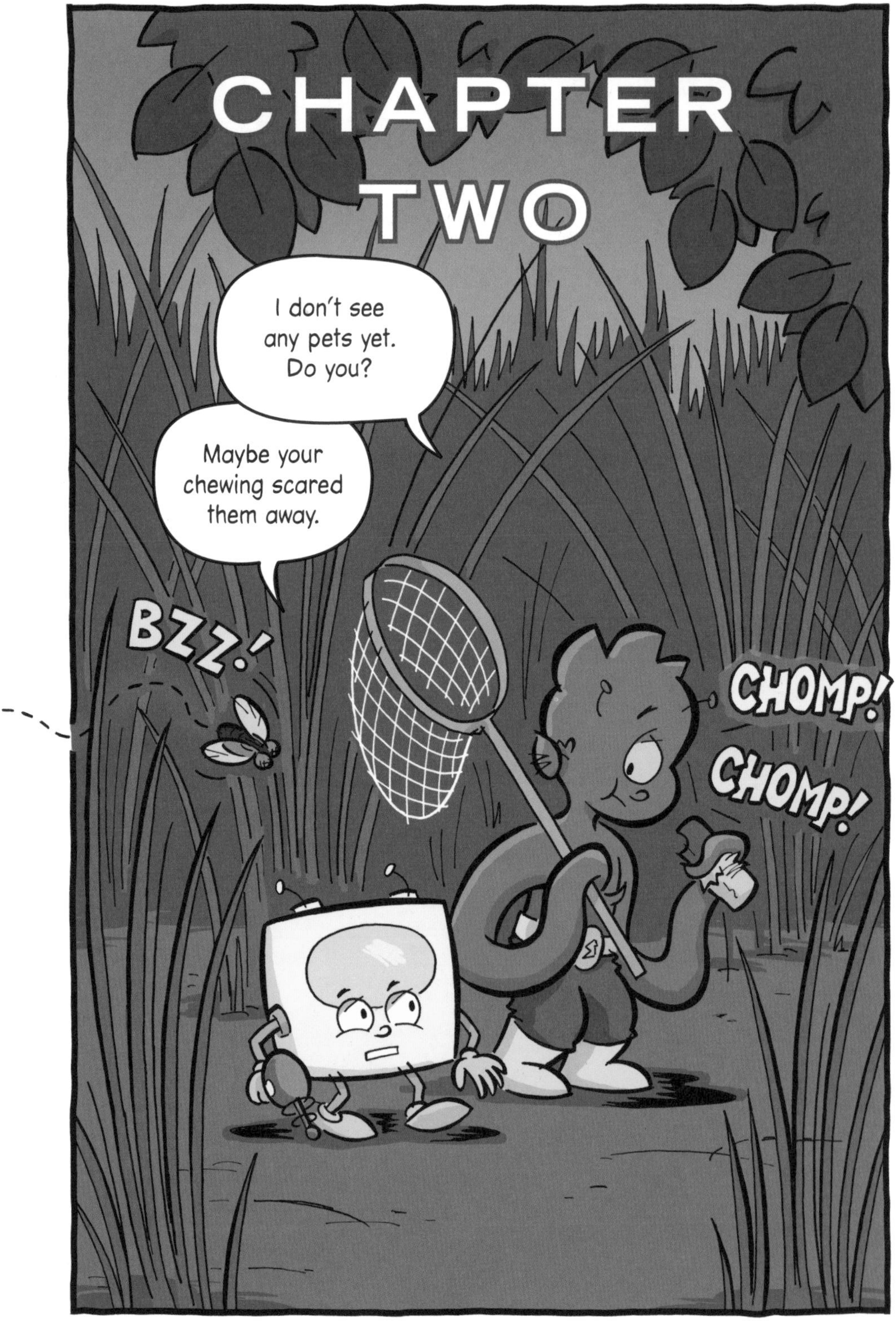
CHAPTER TWO
I don't see any pets yet. Do you?
Maybe your chewing scared them away.
BZZ!
CHOMP!
CHOMP!

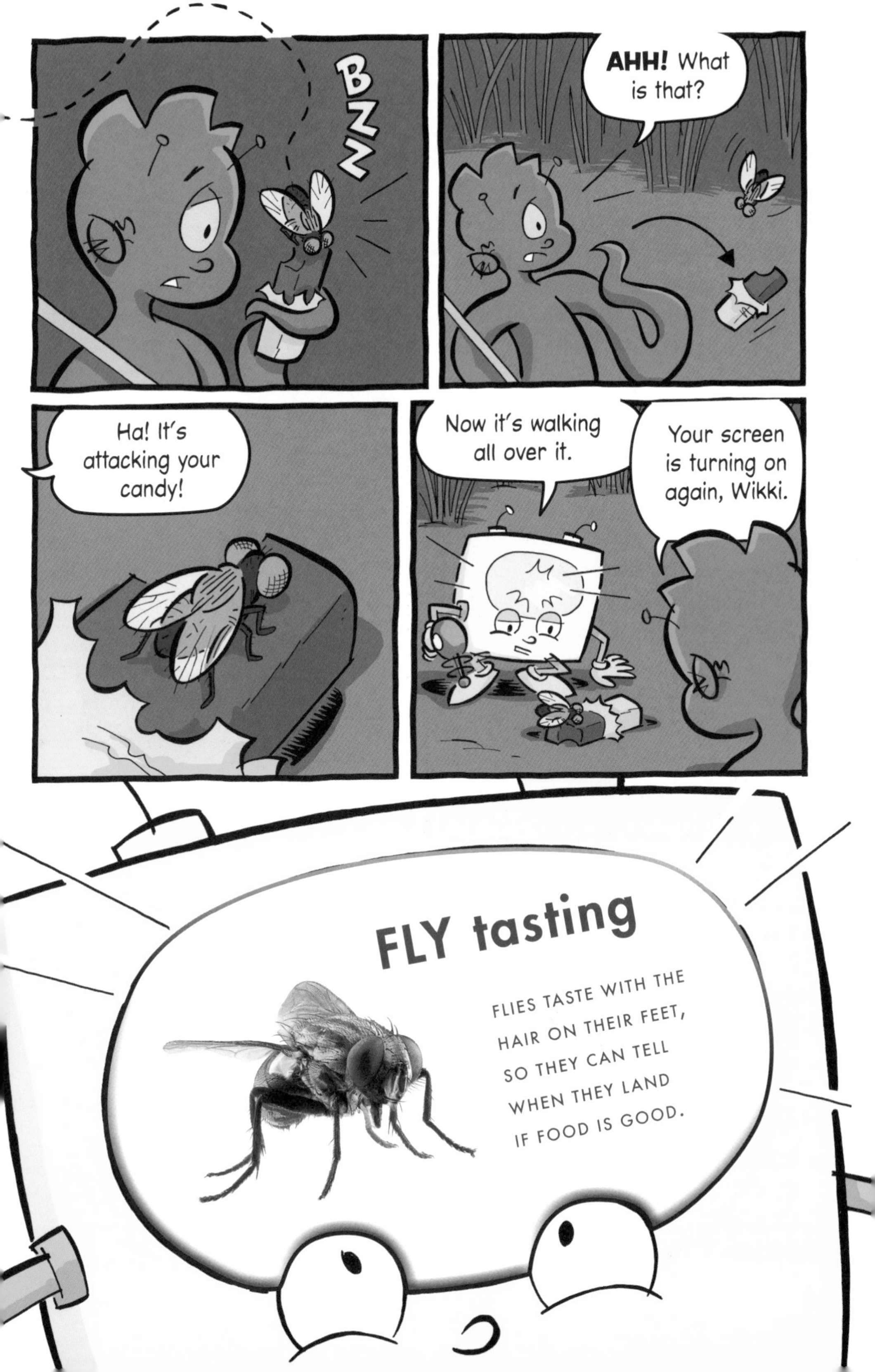
BZZ
AHH! What is that?
Ha! It's attacking your candy!
Now it's walking all over it.
Your screen is turning on again, Wikki.
FLY tasting
FLIES TASTE WITH THE HAIR ON THEIR FEET, SO THEY CAN TELL WHEN THEY LAND IF FOOD IS GOOD.

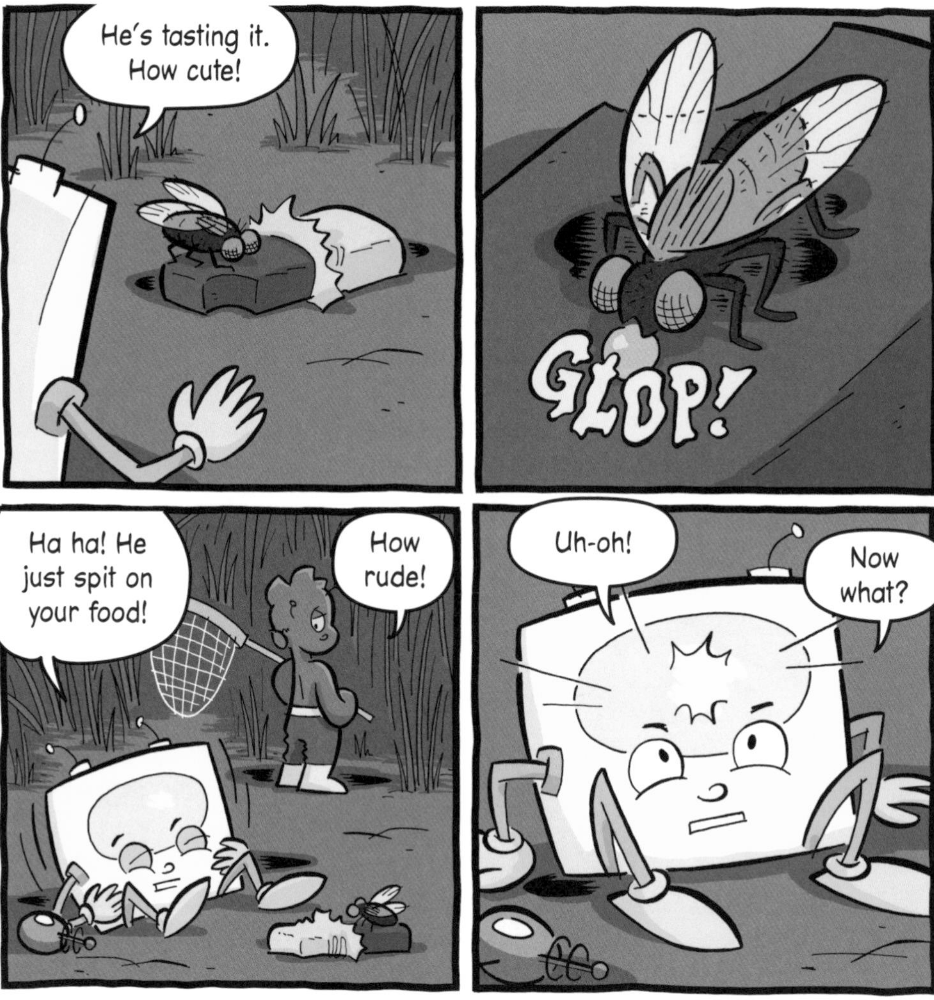
He's tasting it. How cute!
GLOP!
Ha ha! He just spit on your food!
How rude!
Uh-oh!
Now what?

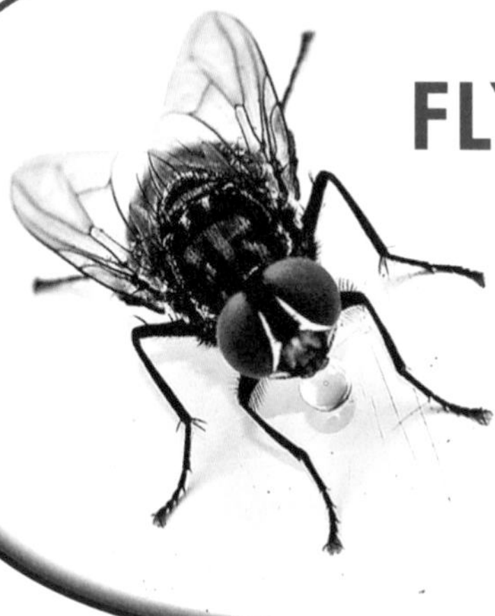

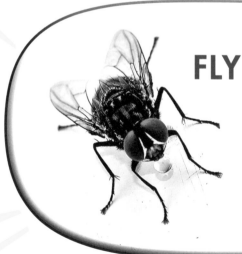

FLY spitting

FLIES USE SPIT TO TURN THEIR FOOD INTO LIQUID, THEN THEY SUCK IT UP AGAIN.

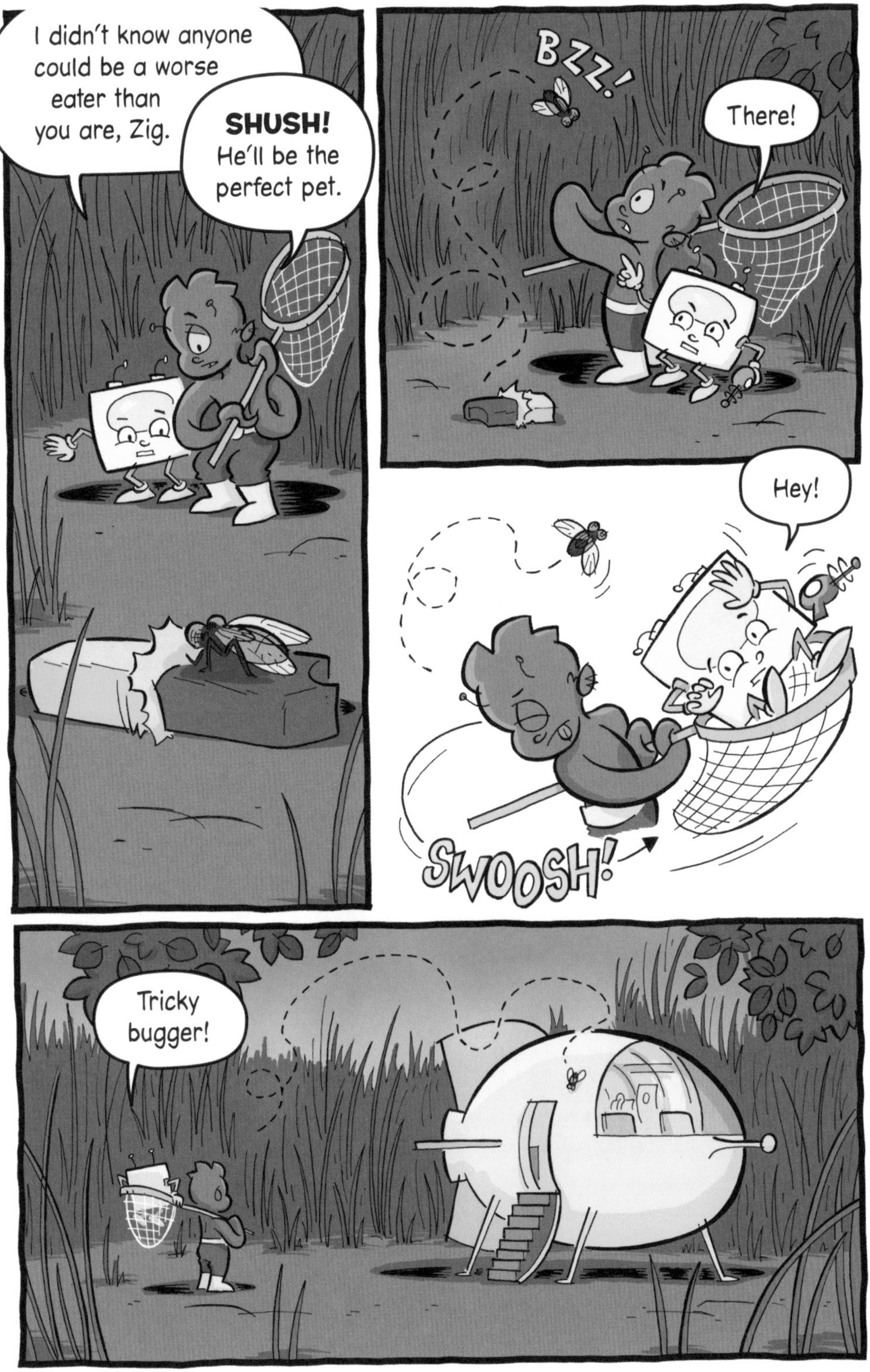
I didn't know anyone could be a worse eater than you are, Zig.
SHUSH! He'll be the perfect pet.
BZZ!
There!
Hey!
SWOOSH!
Tricky bugger!

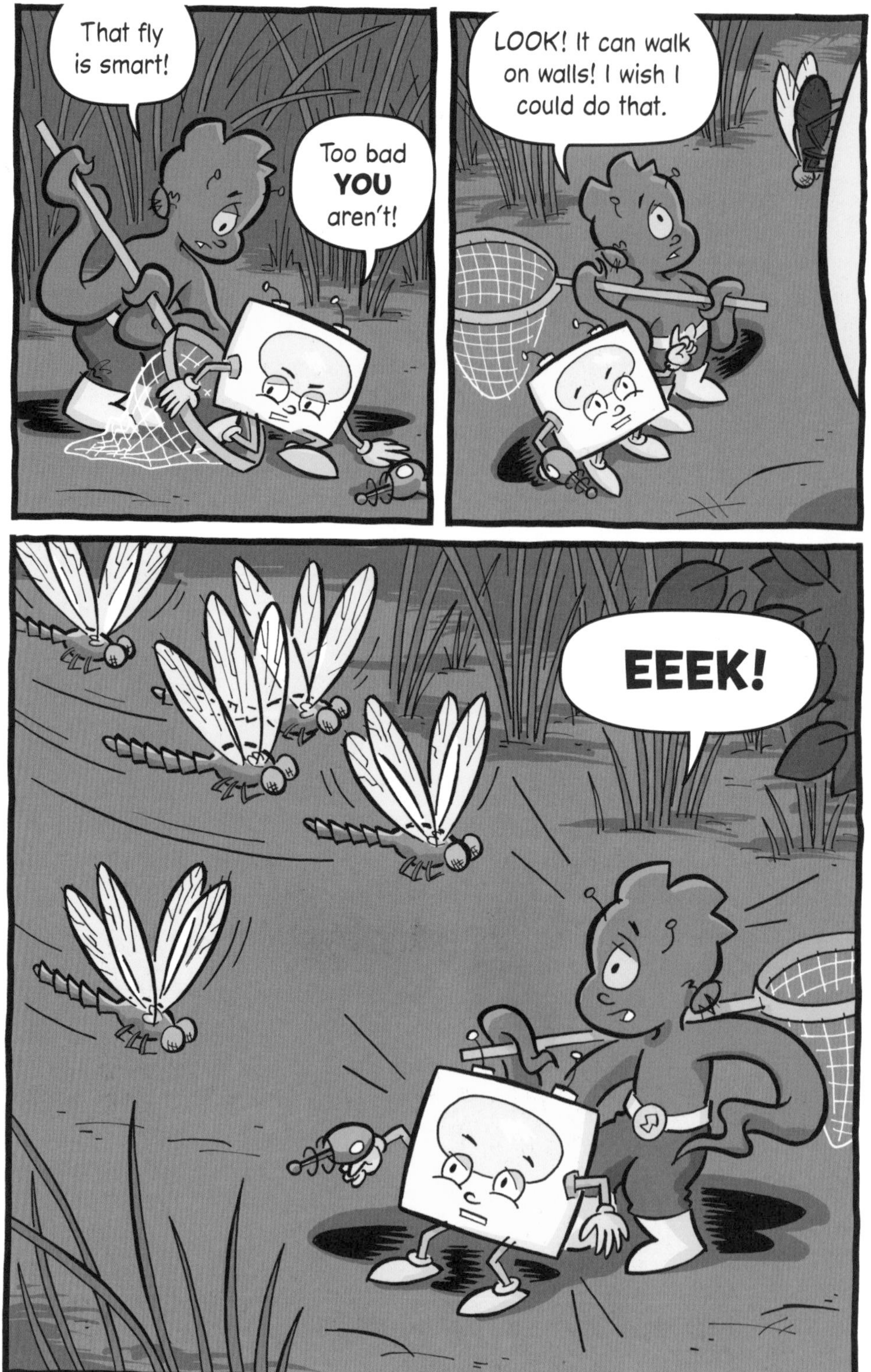
That fly is smart!
Too bad **YOU** aren't!
LOOK! It can walk on walls! I wish I could do that.
EEEK!

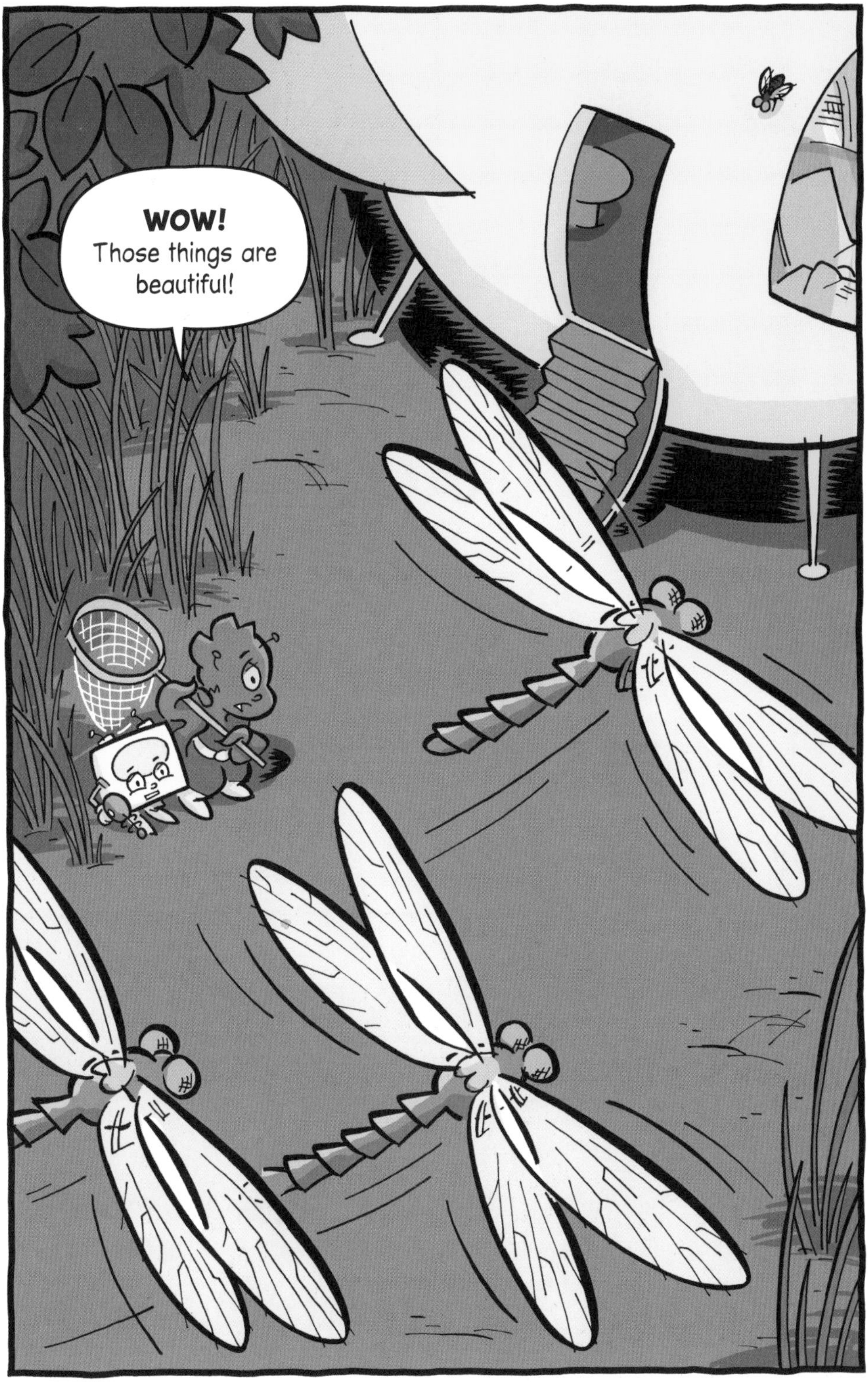
WOW! Those things are beautiful!

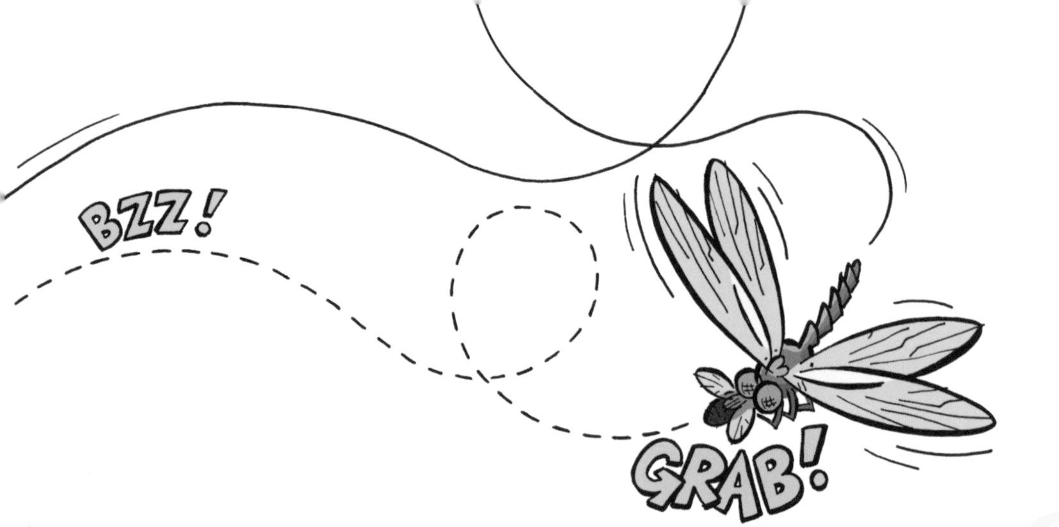
BZZ!
GRAB!

DRAGONFLY

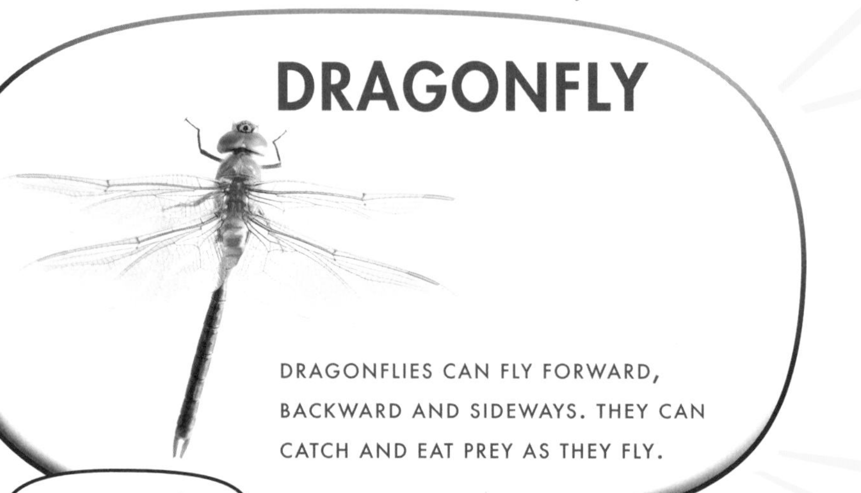

DRAGONFLIES CAN FLY FORWARD, BACKWARD AND SIDEWAYS. THEY CAN CATCH AND EAT PREY AS THEY FLY.

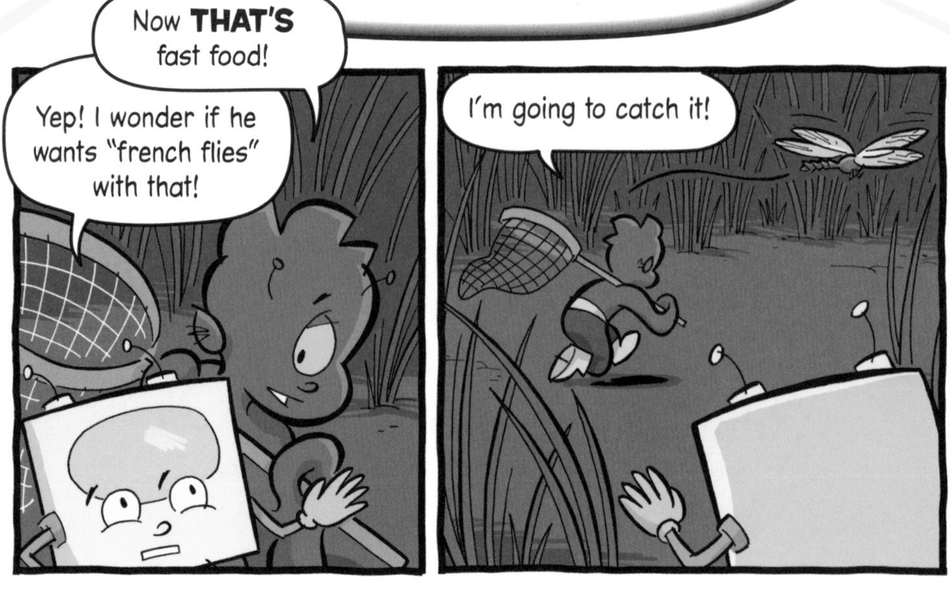
Now **THAT'S** fast food!
Yep! I wonder if he wants "french flies" with that!
I'm going to catch it!

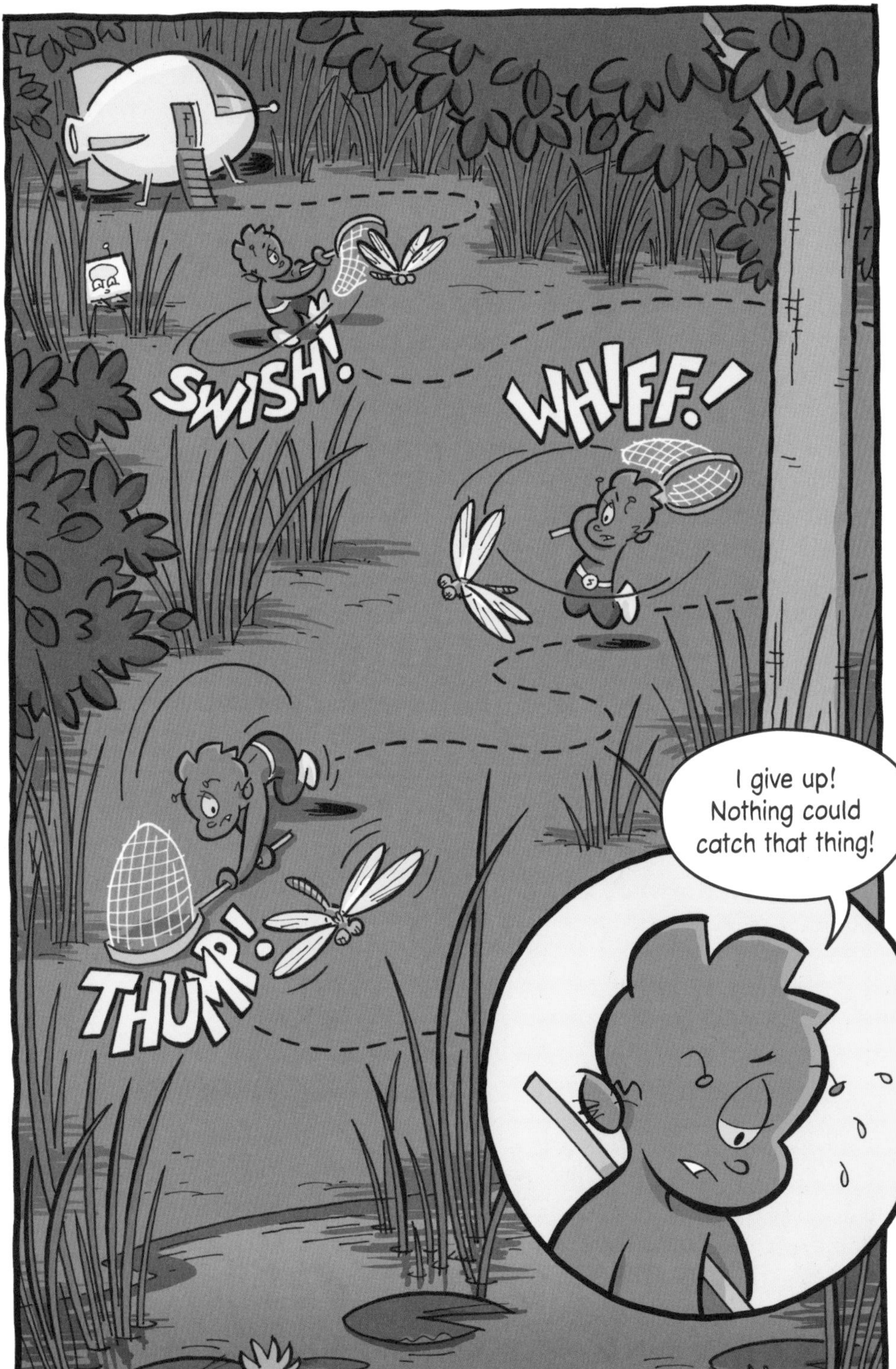
SWISH!
WHIFF!
THUMP!
I give up! Nothing could catch that thing!

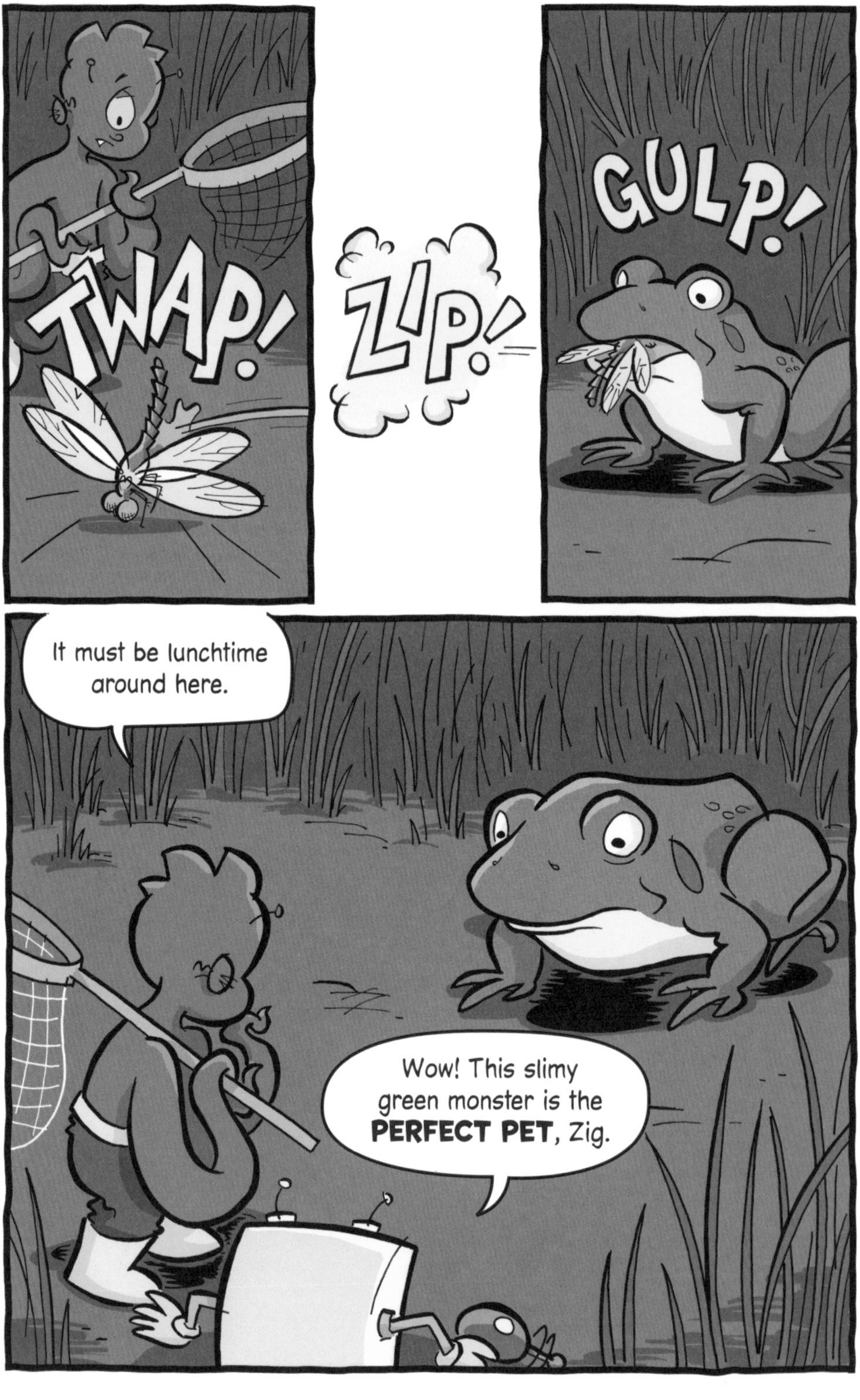
TWAP!
ZIP!
GULP!
It must be lunchtime around here.
Wow! This slimy green monster is the **PERFECT PET**, Zig.

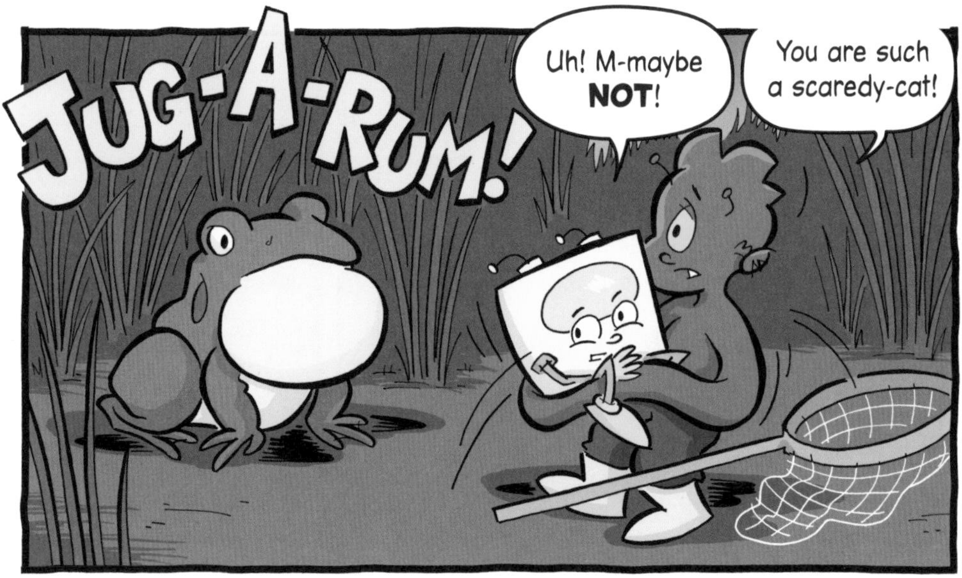
JUG-A-RUM!
Uh! M-maybe NOT!
You are such a scaredy-cat!

FROG croaking

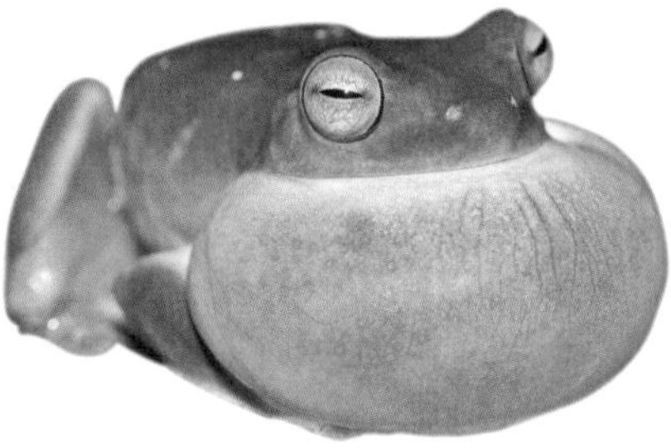

MALE FROGS CROAK TO PROTECT THEIR HOMES AND TO CALL TO LADY FROGS.

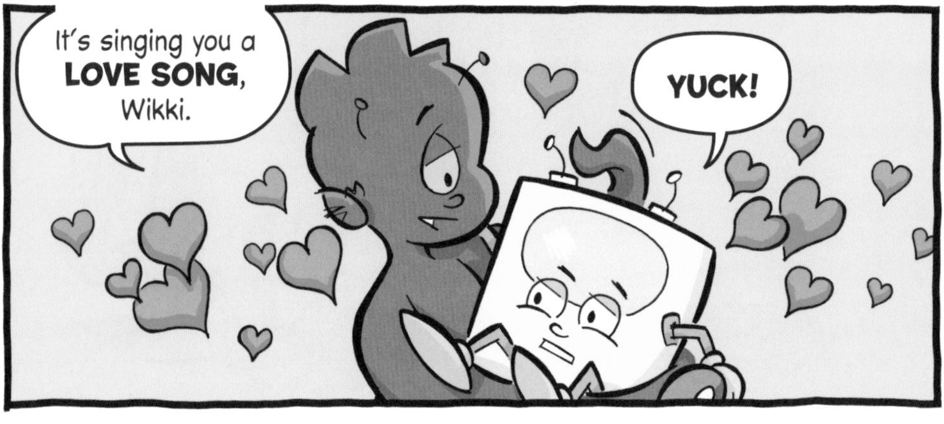
It's singing you a LOVE SONG, Wikki.
YUCK!

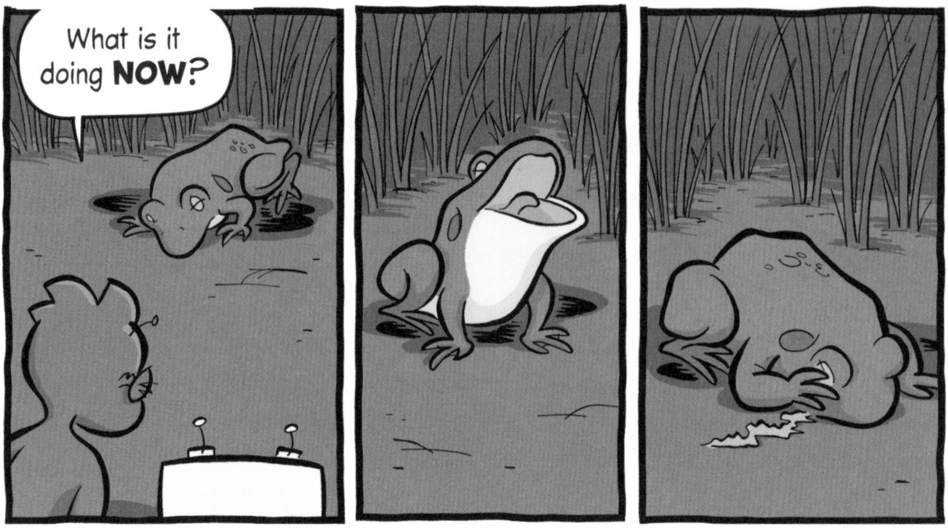
What is it doing **NOW**?

FROG eating its skin

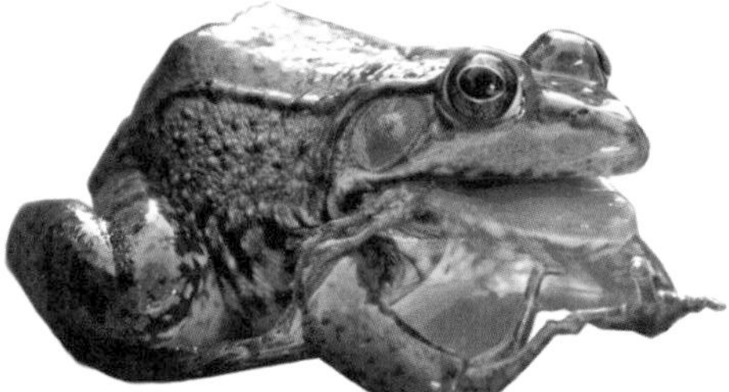

SOME FROGS SHED THEIR SKIN ABOUT ONCE A WEEK. AND THEN THEY EAT IT.

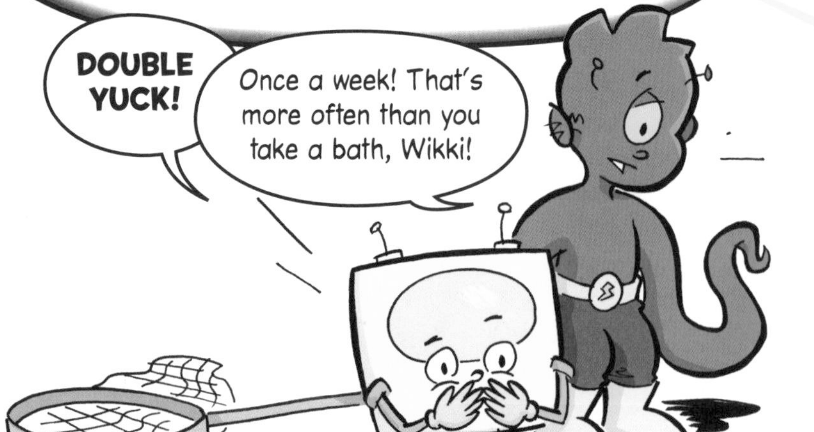
DOUBLE YUCK!
Once a week! That's more often than you take a bath, Wikki!

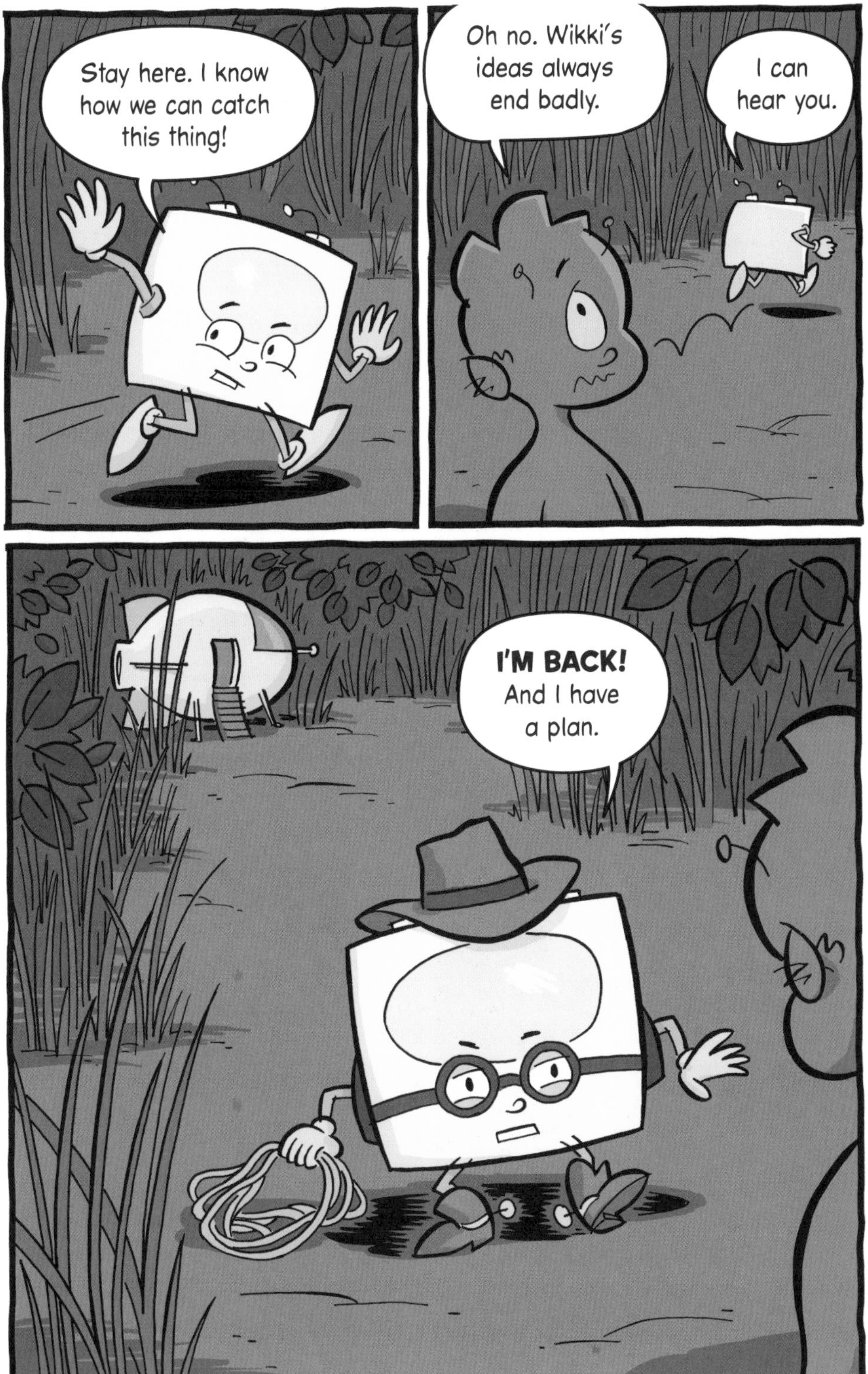
Stay here. I know how we can catch this thing!
Oh no. Wikki's ideas always end badly.
I can hear you.
I'M BACK! And I have a plan.

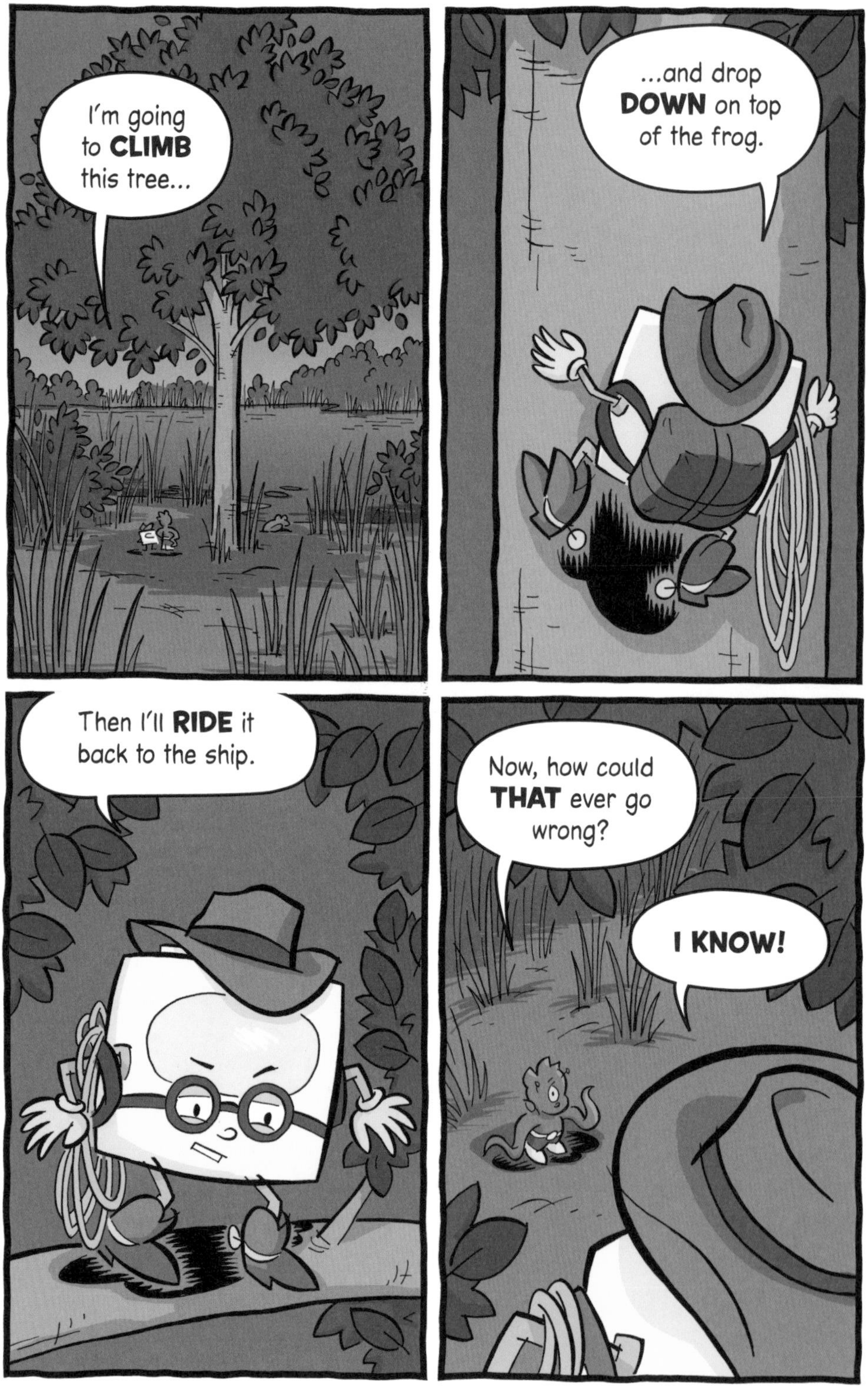
I'm going to **CLIMB** this tree...
...and drop **DOWN** on top of the frog.
Then I'll **RIDE** it back to the ship.
Now, how could **THAT** ever go wrong?
I KNOW!

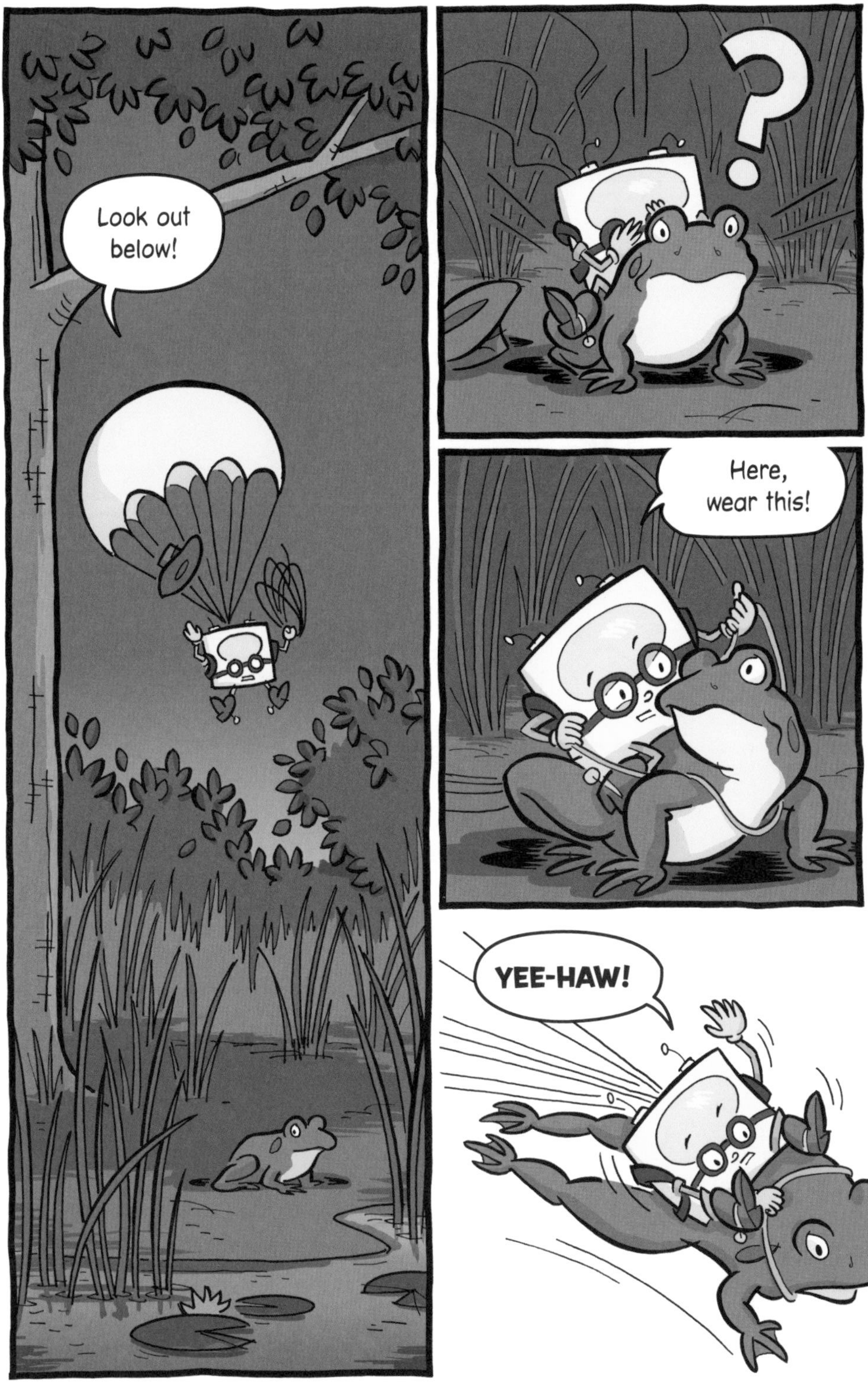
Look out below!
?
Here, wear this!
YEE-HAW!

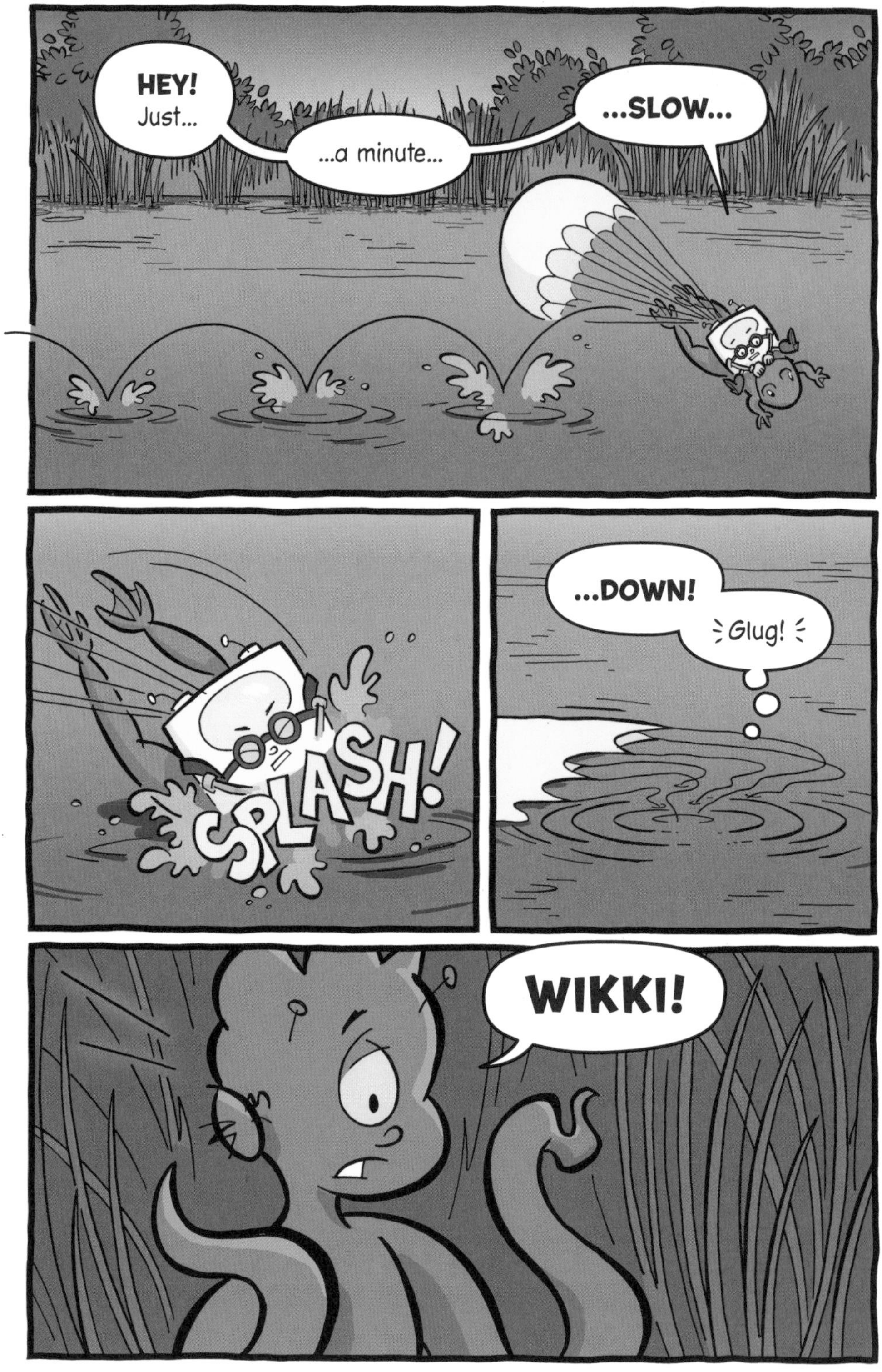
HEY! Just...
...a minute...
...SLOW...
SPLASH!
...DOWN!
Glug!
WIKKI!

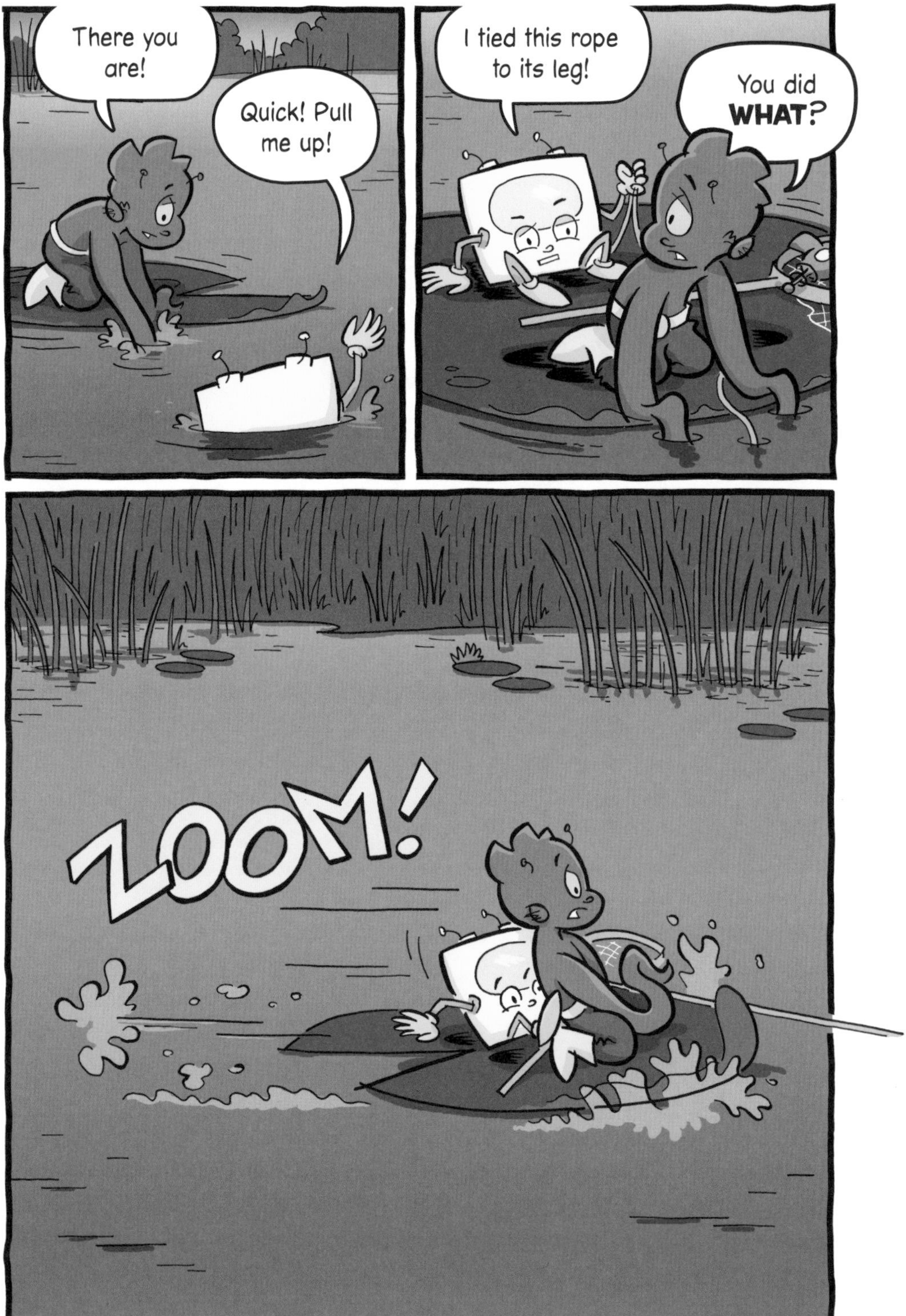
There you are!
Quick! Pull me up!
I tied this rope to its leg!
You did **WHAT?**
ZOOM!

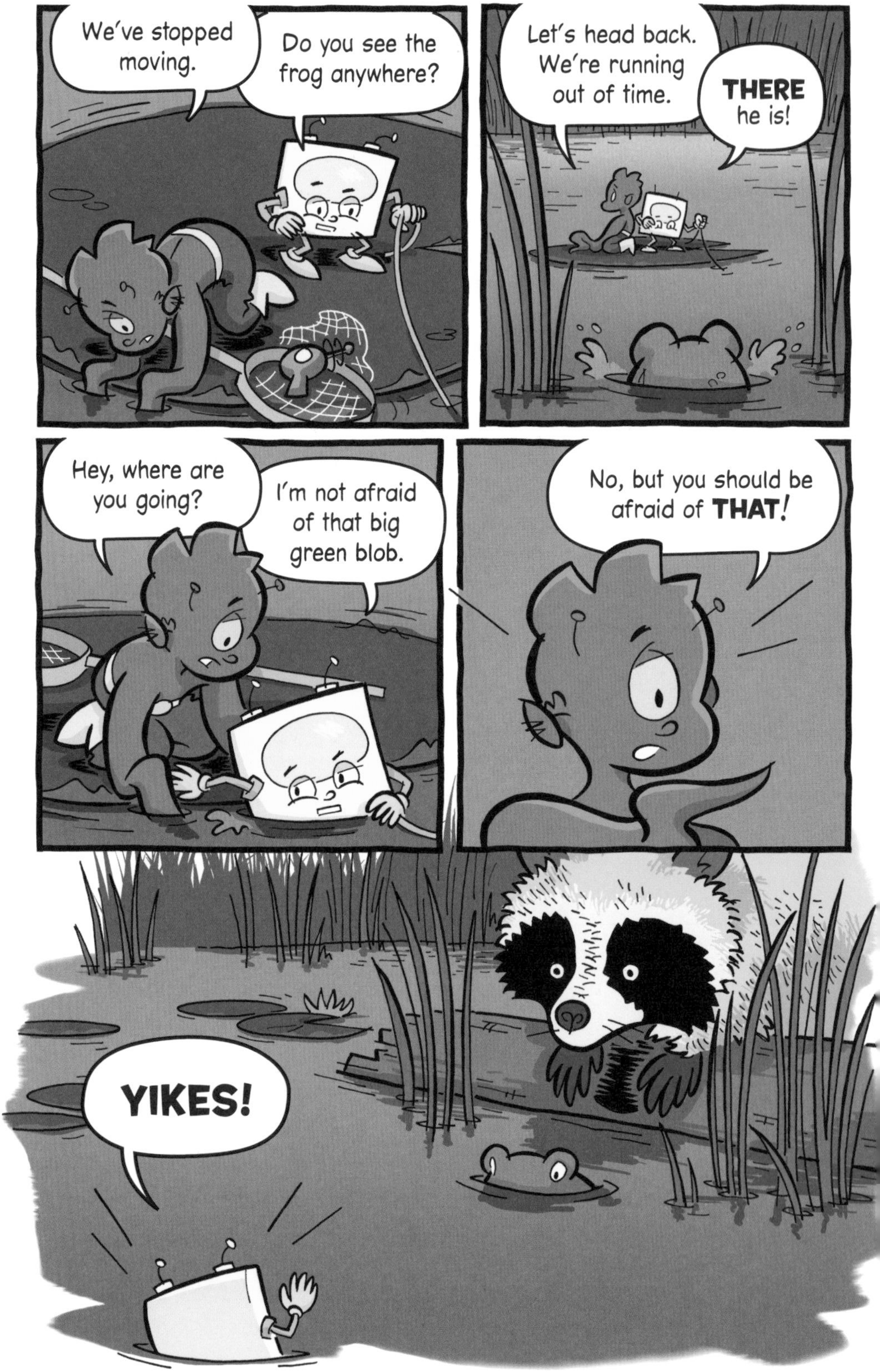
We've stopped moving.
Do you see the frog anywhere?
Let's head back. We're running out of time.
THERE he is!
Hey, where are you going?
I'm not afraid of that big green blob.
No, but you should be afraid of THAT!
YIKES!

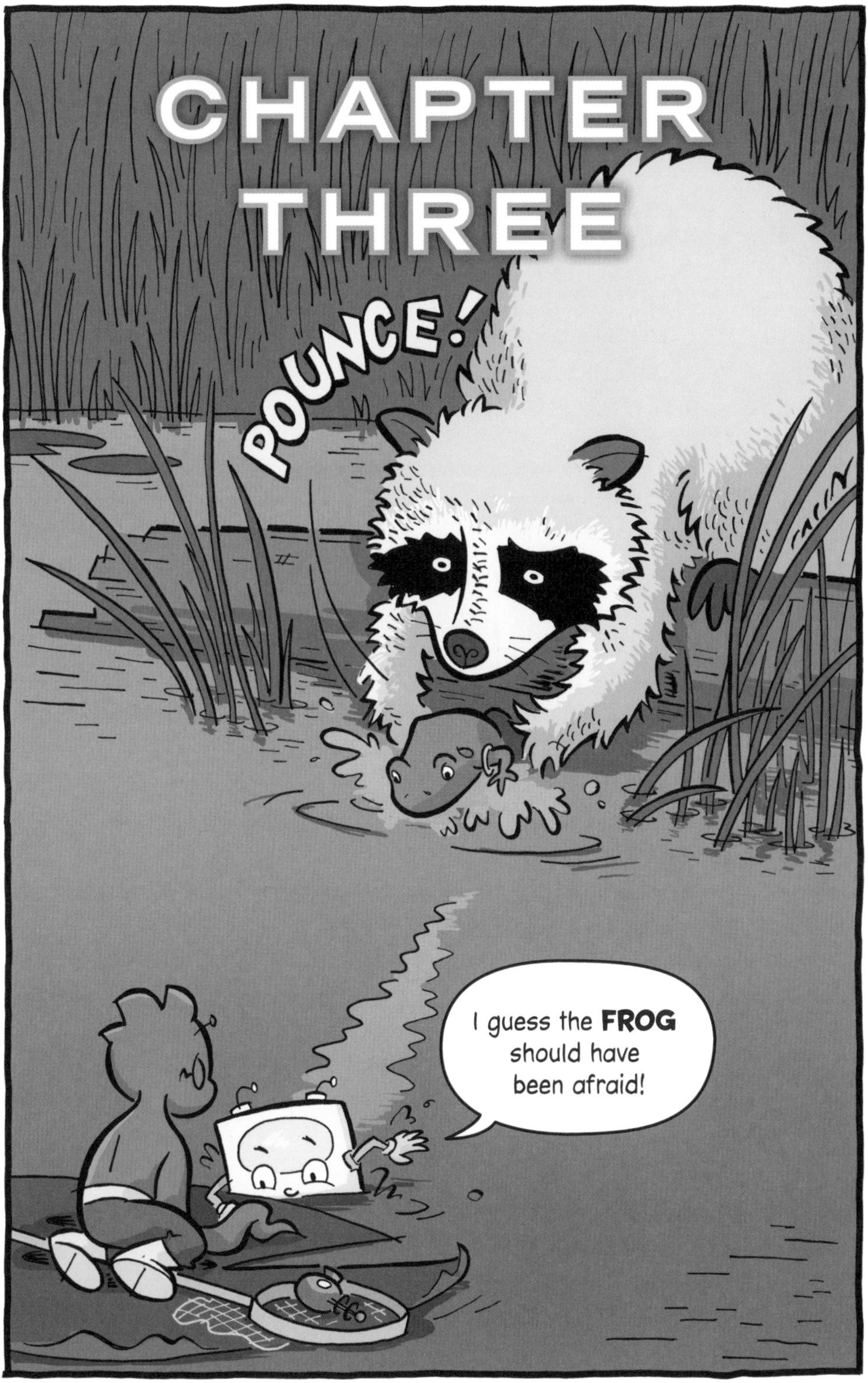
CHAPTER THREE
POUNCE!
I guess the **FROG** should have been afraid!

RACCOON hand

RACCOONS HAVE FIVE
FINGERS ON EACH HAND,
WHICH COME IN HANDY!

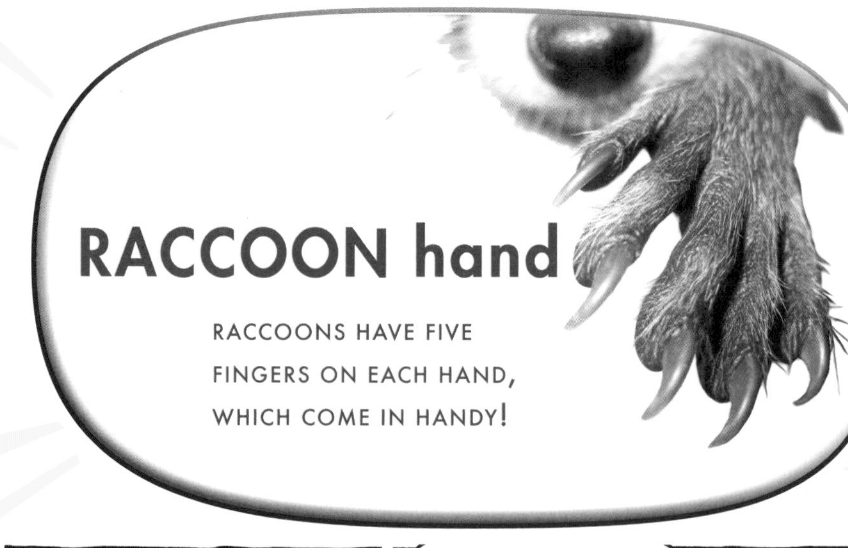

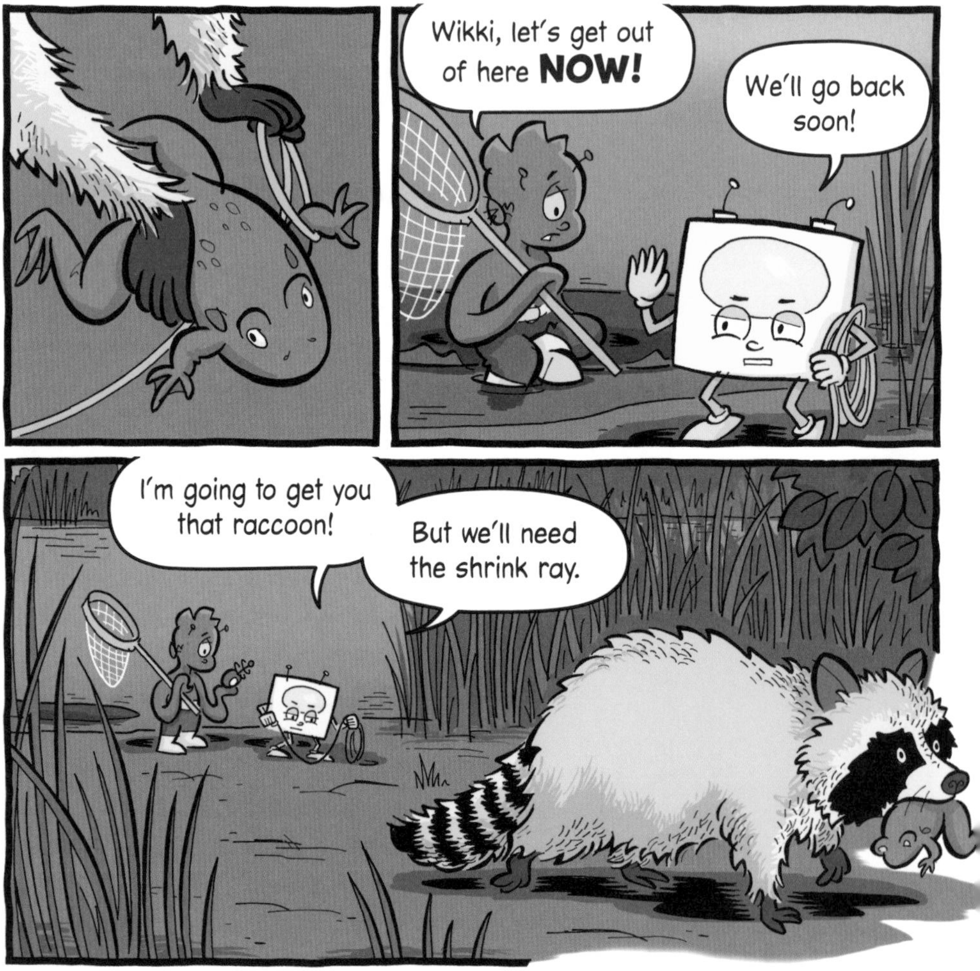

Wikki, let's get out of here **NOW!**
We'll go back soon!
I'm going to get you that raccoon!
But we'll need the shrink ray.

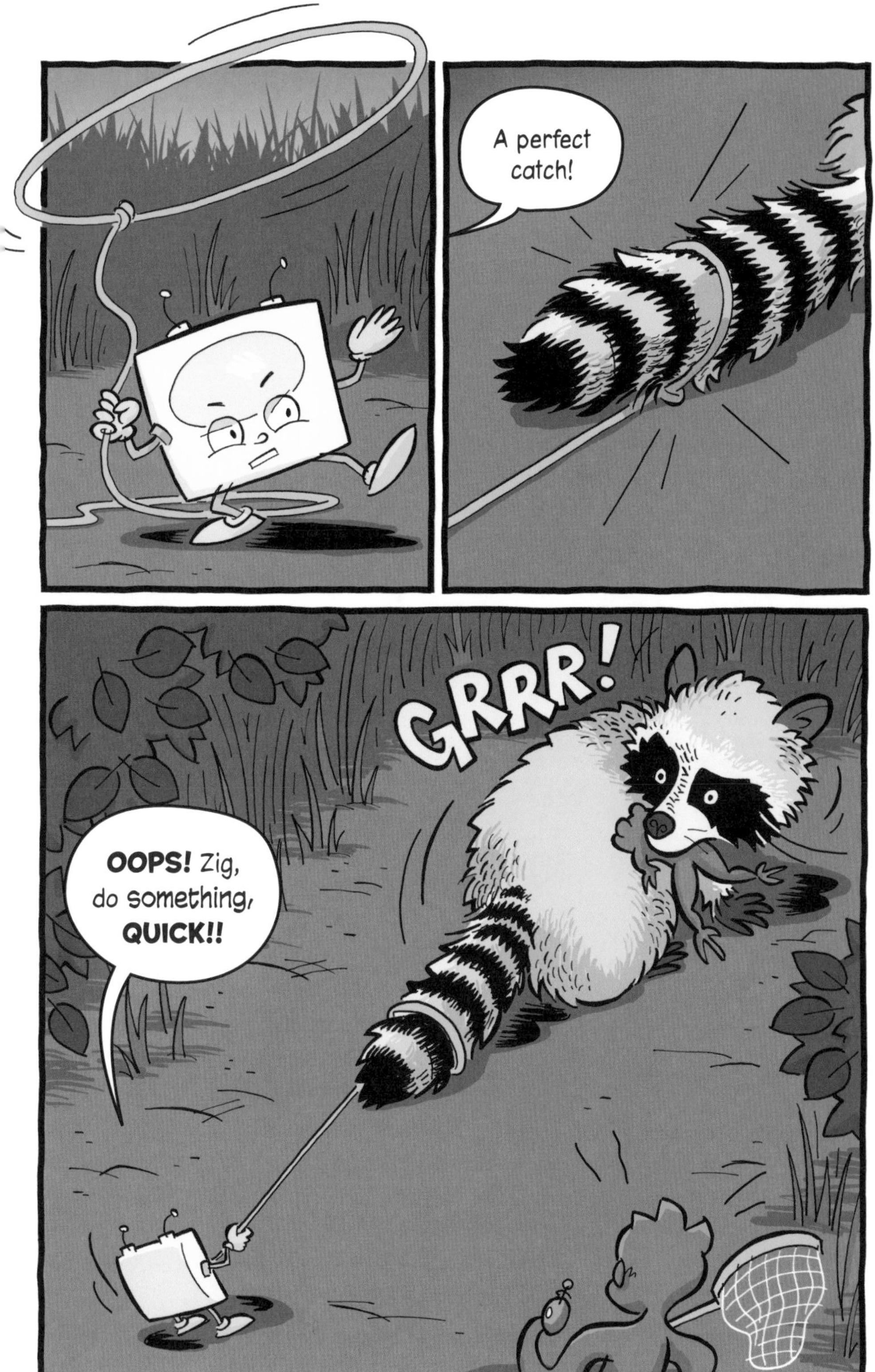
A perfect catch!
GRRR!
OOPS! Zig, do something, QUICK!!

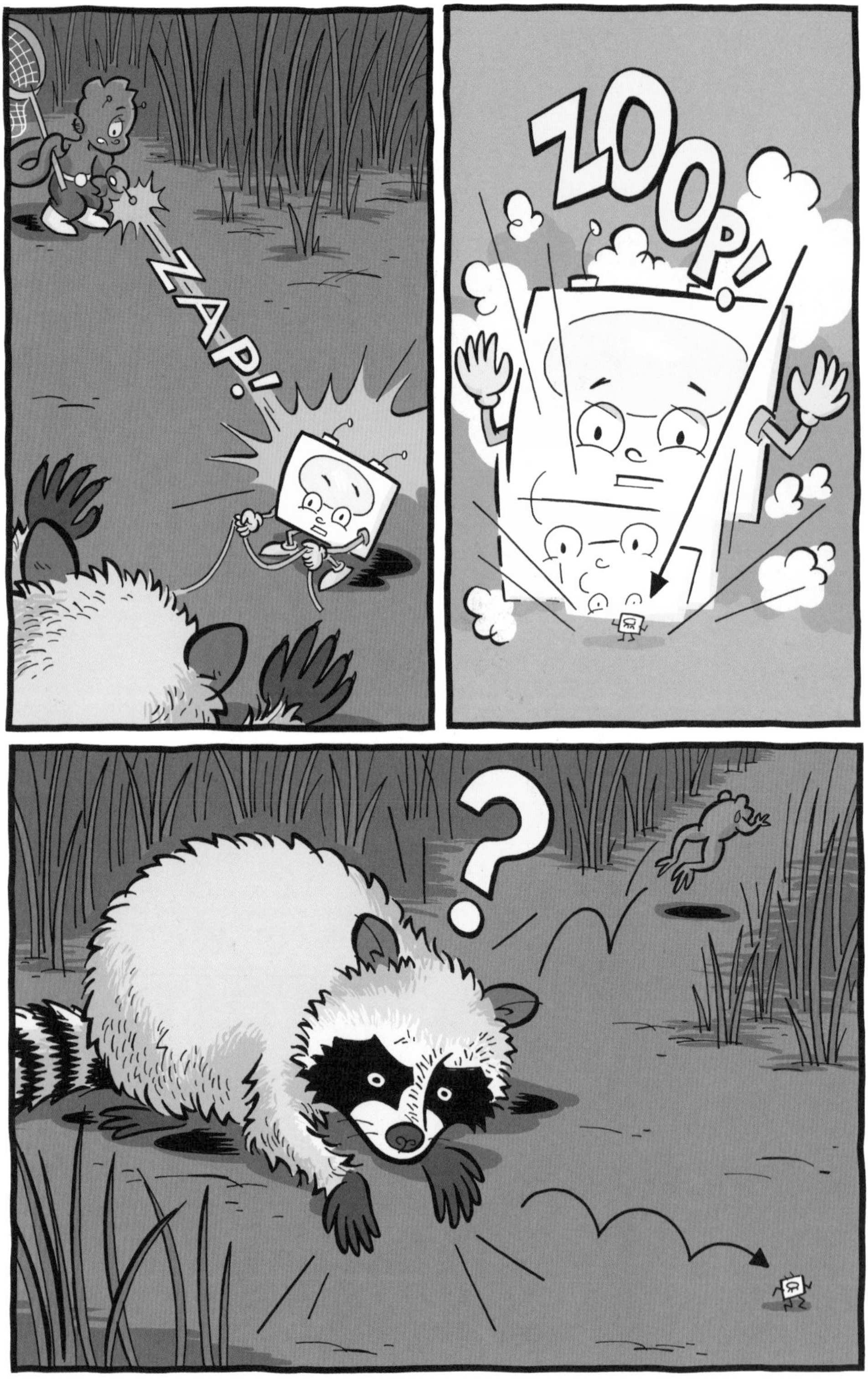
ZAP!
ZOOP!
?

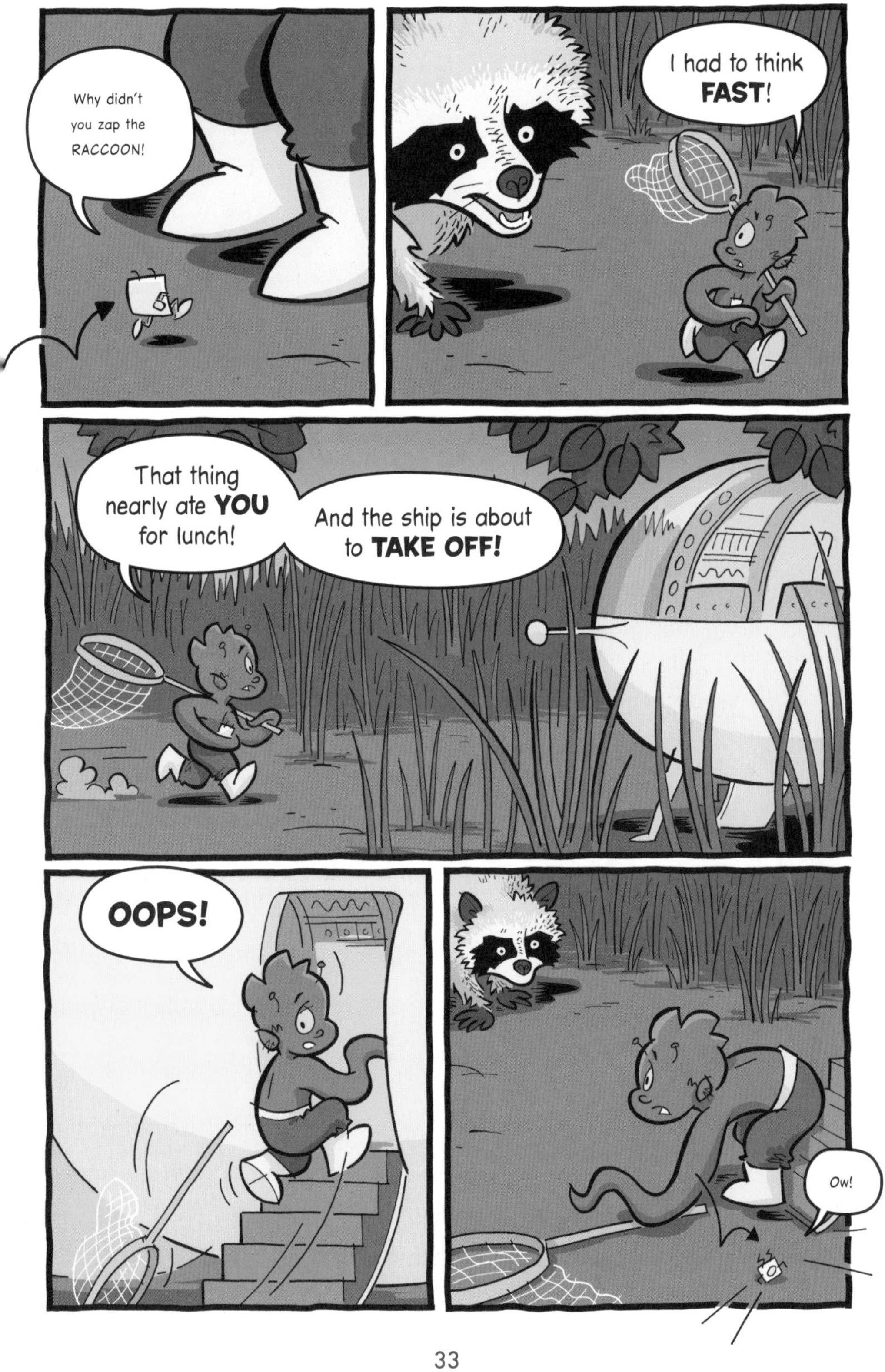
Why didn't you zap the RACCOON!
I had to think FAST!
That thing nearly ate YOU for lunch!
And the ship is about to TAKE OFF!
OOPS!
Ow!

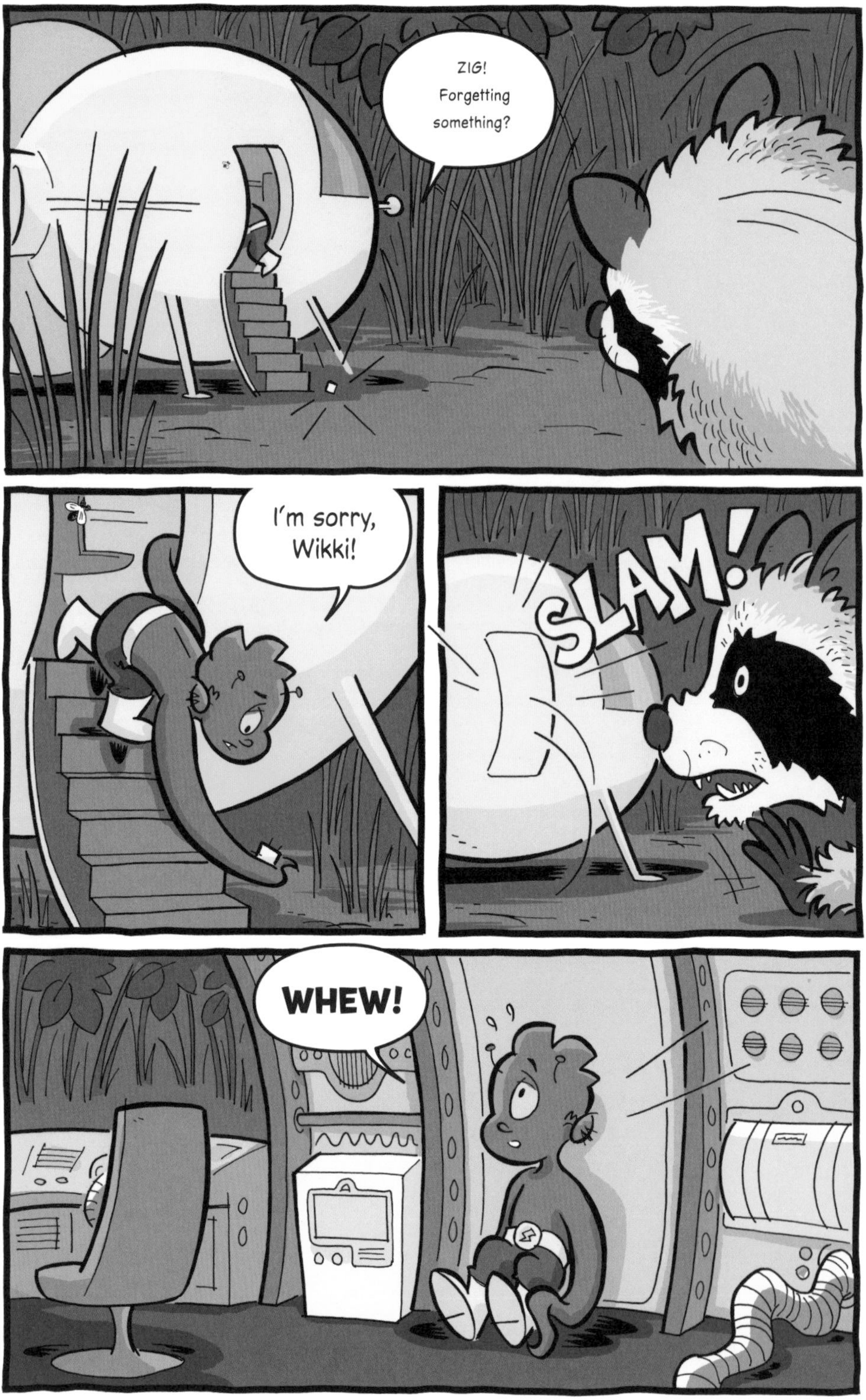

ZIG! Forgetting something?
I'm sorry, Wikki!
SLAM!
WHEW!

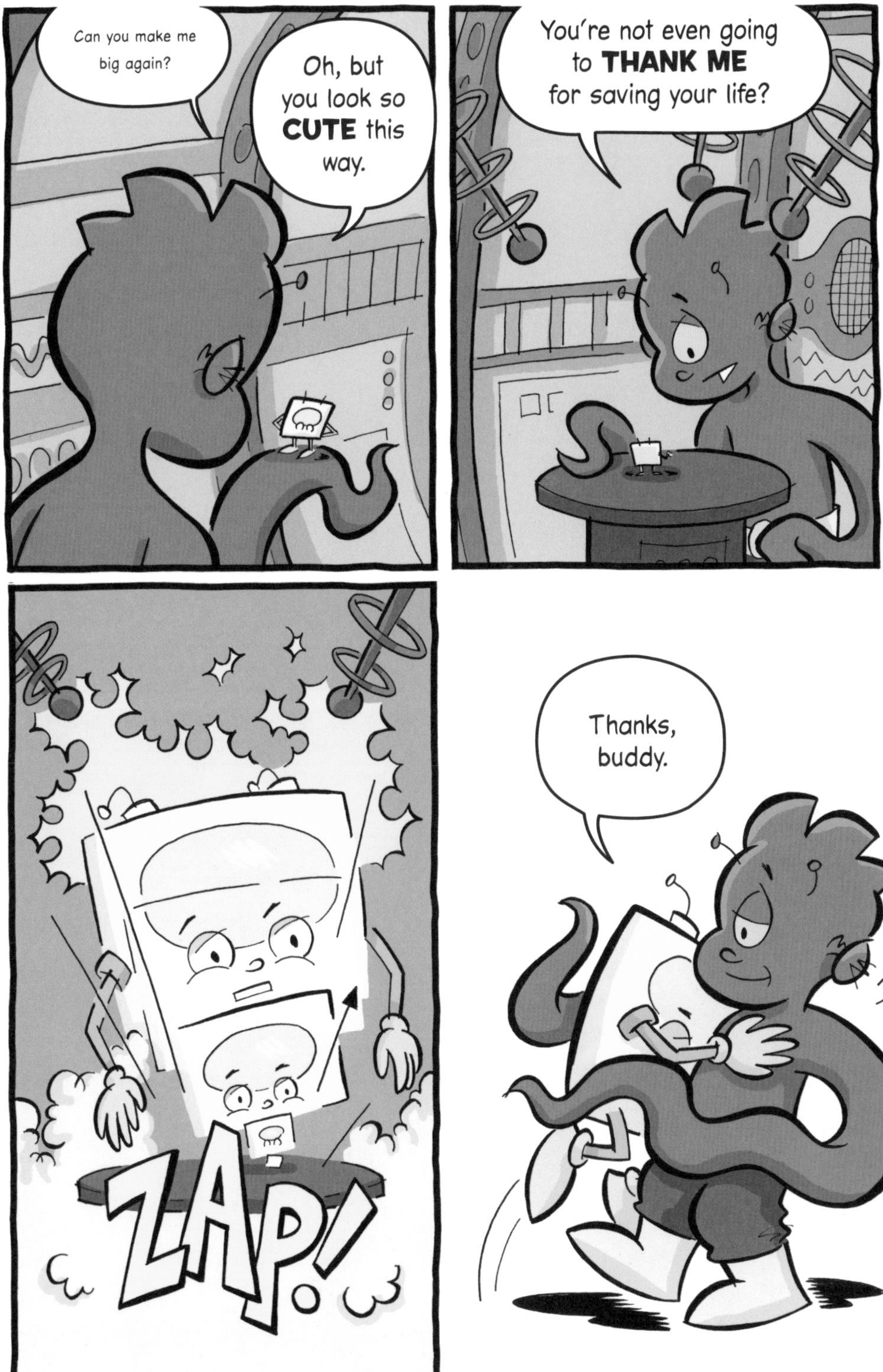
Can you make me big again?
Oh, but you look so **CUTE** this way.
You're not even going to **THANK ME** for saving your life?
ZAP!
Thanks, buddy.

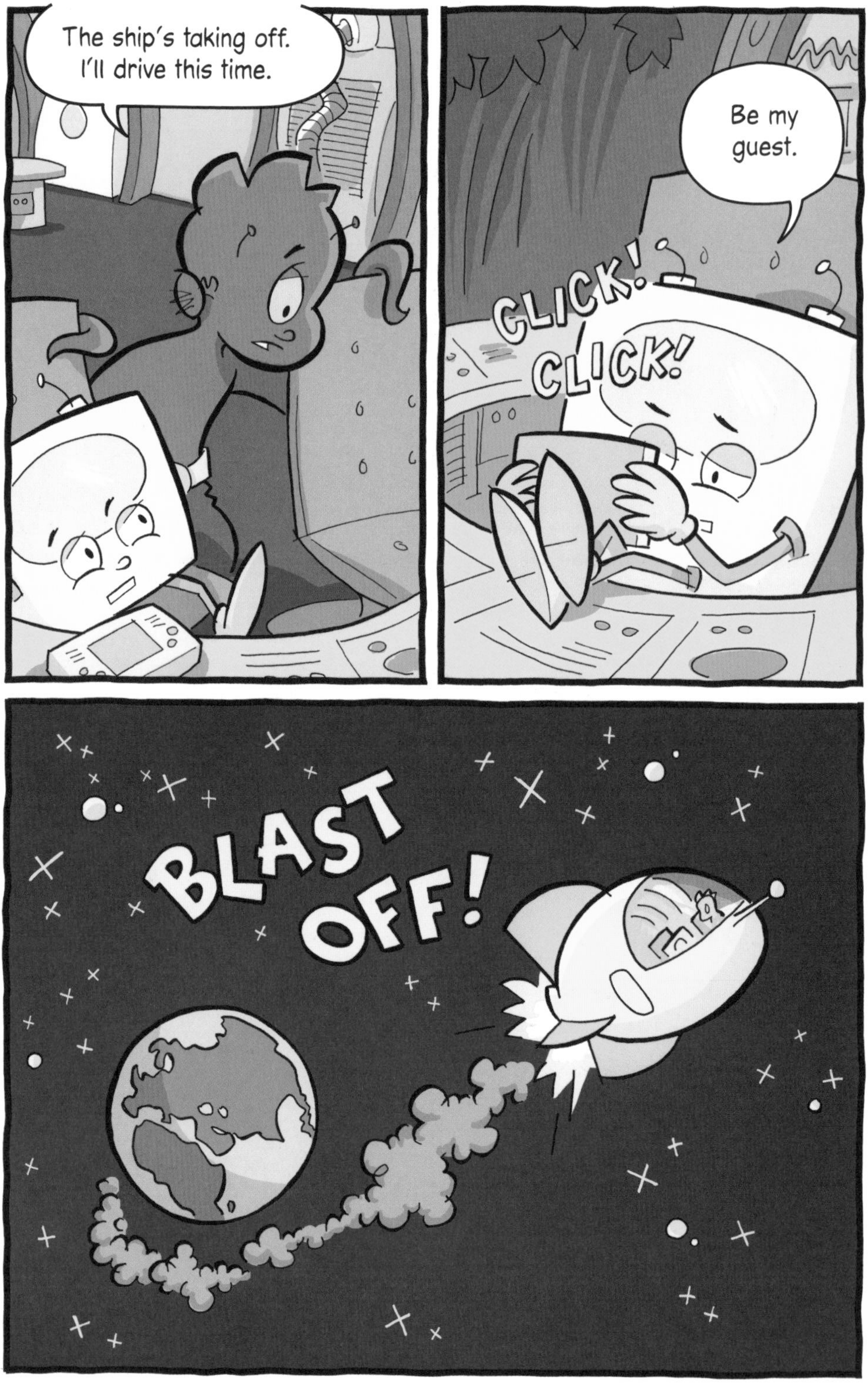
The ship's taking off. I'll drive this time.
Be my guest.
CLICK!
CLICK!
BLAST OFF!

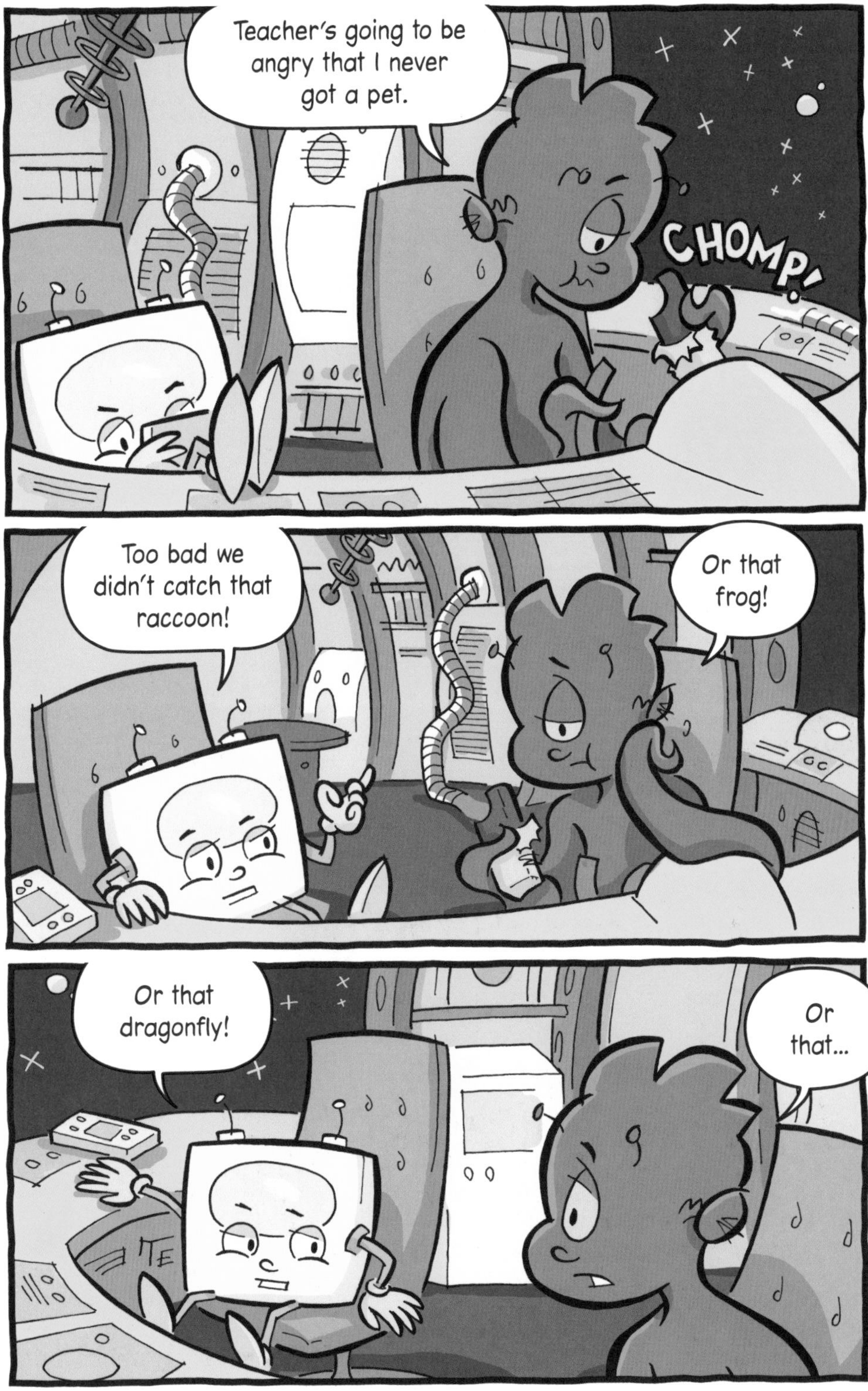
Teacher's going to be angry that I never got a pet.
CHOMP!
Too bad we didn't catch that raccoon!
Or that frog!
Or that dragonfly!
Or that...

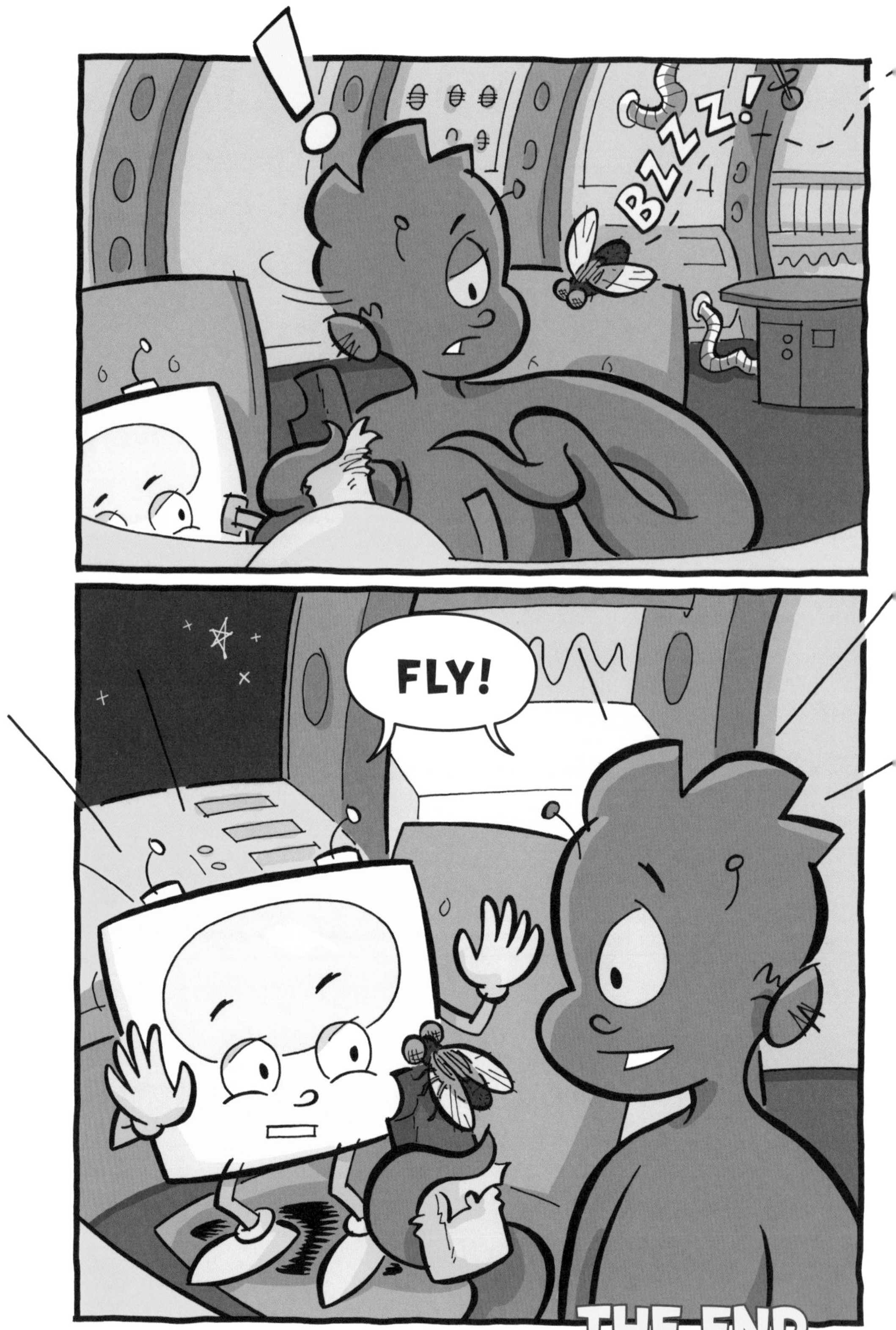

!
BZZZZ!
FLY!
THE END

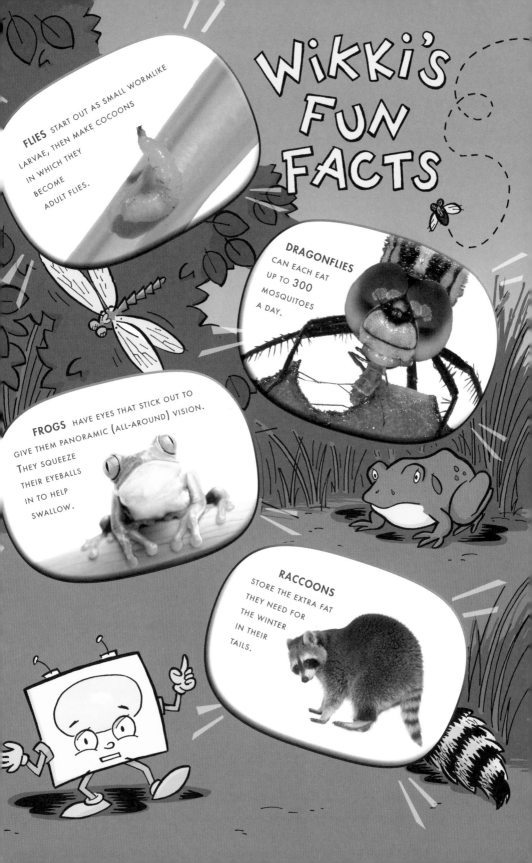

Wikki's Fun Facts

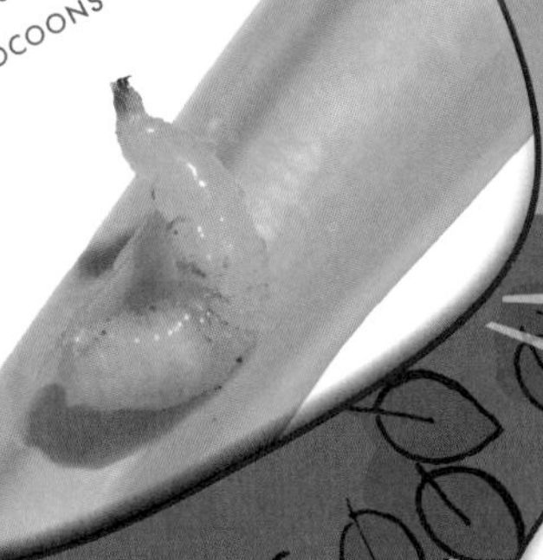

FLIES start out as small wormlike larvae, then make cocoons in which they become adult flies.

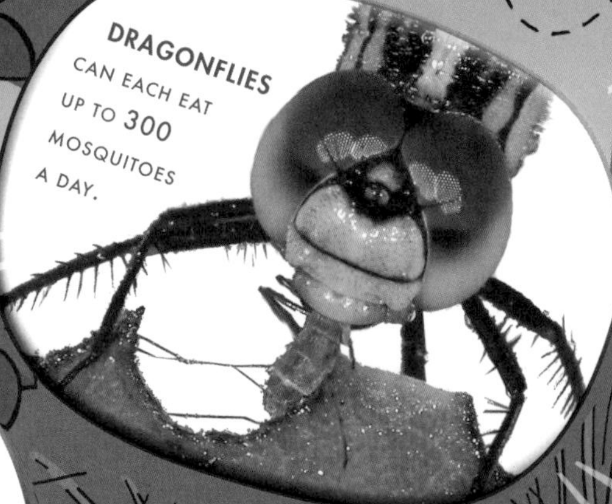

DRAGONFLIES can each eat up to 300 mosquitoes a day.

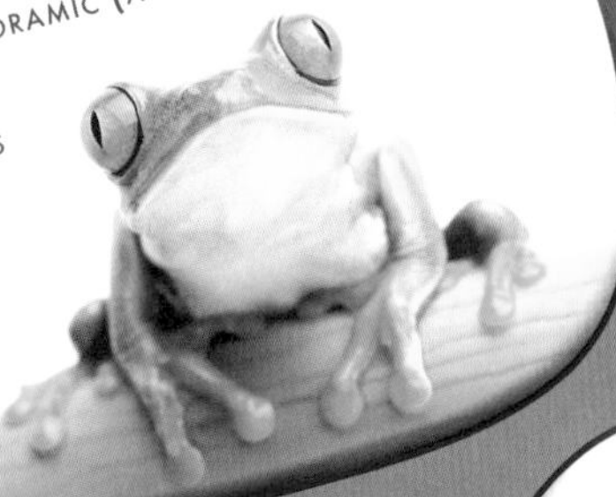

FROGS have eyes that stick out to give them panoramic (all-around) vision. They squeeze their eyeballs in to help swallow.

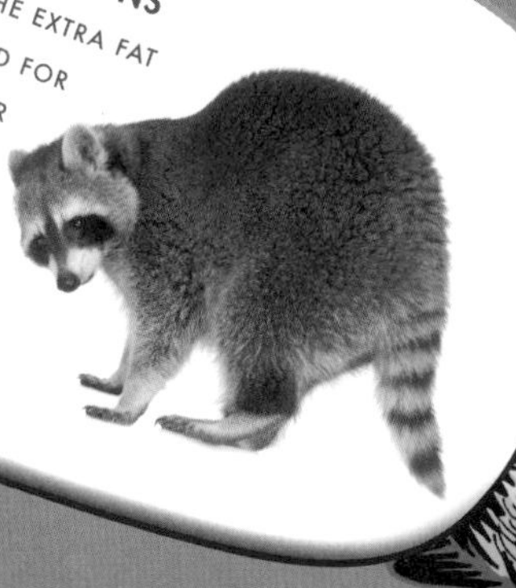

RACCOONS store the extra fat they need for the winter in their tails.

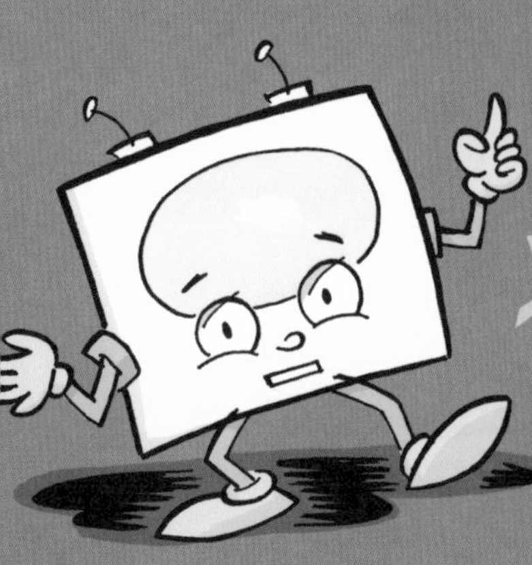

ABOUT THE AUTHORS

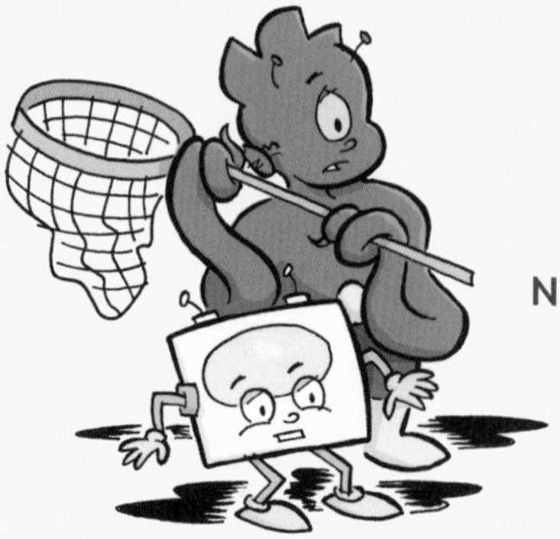

NADJA SPIEGELMAN, who wrote Zig and Wikki's story, graduated from Yale University as an English major. She grew up in New York City where there are few dragonflies and frogs, although there are certainly plenty of houseflies. When she was younger, she loved going to the country, where she collected insects and salamanders and kept them inside her shoe-box "bug museum."

TRADE LOEFFLER, who drew Zig and Wikki, grew up in Livermore, California. Unlike Zig and Wikki, he doesn't believe flies make good pets. But he did like to collect them when he was a kid—to feed them to the funnel spiders that lived in a field near his house. Trade now lives in New York City with his wife, Annalisa; son, Clark; and dog, Boo. He is the creator of the all-ages web comic *Zip and Li'l Bit.*

HOW TO "TOON INTO READING"

in a few simple steps:

Our goal is to get kids reading—and we know kids LOVE comics. We publish award-winning early readers in comics form for elementary and early middle school, and present them in three levels.

CHICK & CHICKIE
PLAY ALL DAY!
What do you want to play?
I have a great idea...
Claude Ponti
ZIG AND WIKKI
MO AND JO
FIGHTING TOGETHER FOREVER
BENNY AND PENNY
THE SHARK KING

① FIND THE RIGHT BOOK

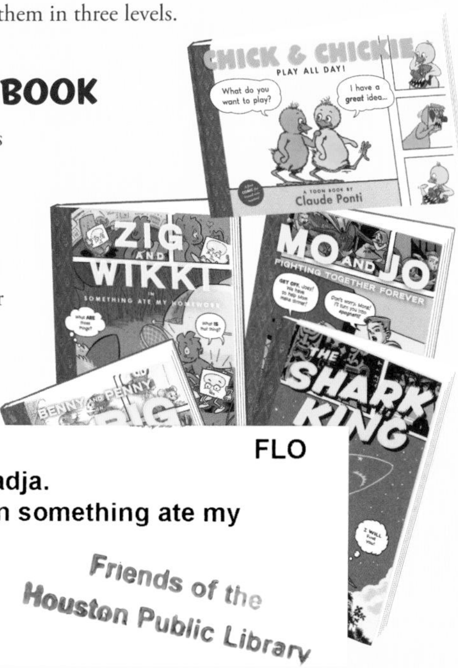

Veteran teacher Cindy Rosado tells what makes a good book for beginning and struggling readers alike: "A vetted vocabulary, plenty of picture clues, repetition, and a clear and compelling story. Also, the book shouldn't be too easy—or the reader won't learn, but neither should it be too hard—or he or she may get discouraged."

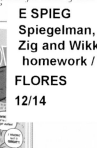

If you love Zig and Wikki, look for more of their adventures in "The Cow!"

ZIG AND WIKKI in
THE COW
I KNOW! Isn't it GREAT?!
NADJA SPIEGELMAN & TRADE LOEFFLER

ZIG AND WIKKI
in The Cow
by Nadja Spiegelman & Trade Loeffler

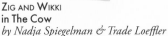

The TOON INTO READING!™ program is designed for beginning readers and works wonders with reluctant readers.

② TAKE TIME WITH SILENT PANELS

Comics use panels to mark time, and silent panels count. Look and "read" even when there are no words. Often, humor is all in the timing!

KNOCK! KNOCK!
TRICK OR TREAT!

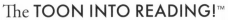

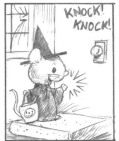

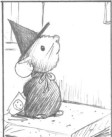

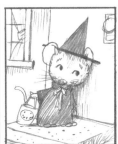

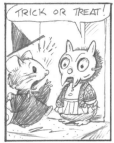

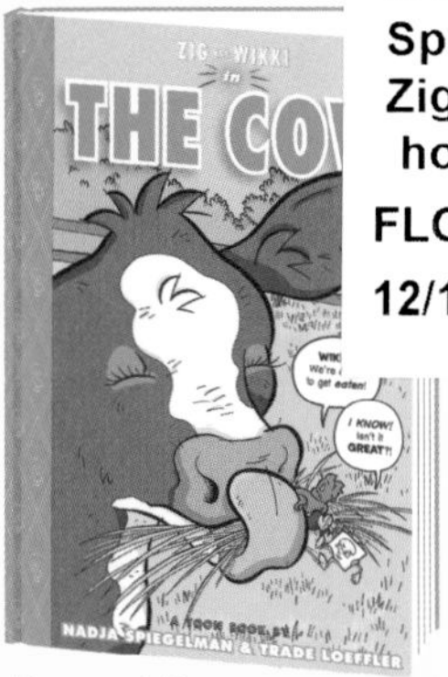

3 GUIDE YOUNG READERS

What works?

Keep your fingertip below the character that is speaking.

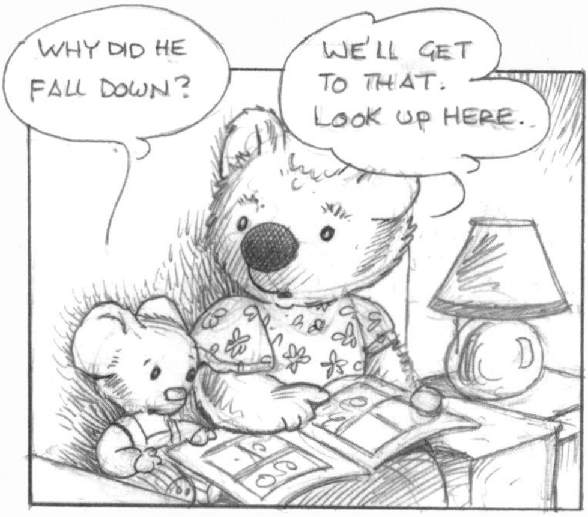
WHY DID HE FALL DOWN?
WE'LL GET TO THAT. LOOK UP HERE.

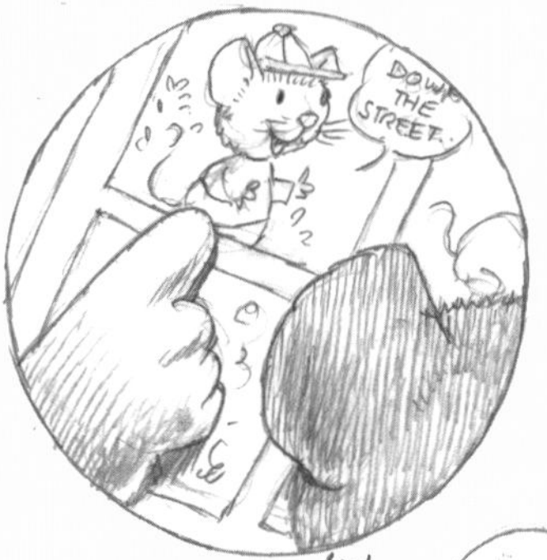
DOWN THE STREET.

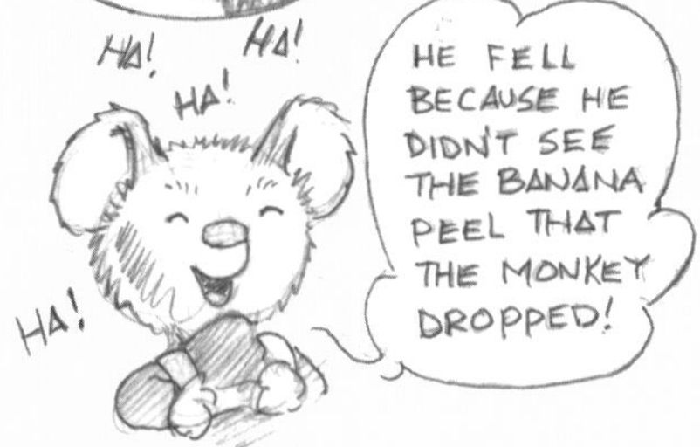
HA! HA! HA! HA!
HE FELL BECAUSE HE DIDN'T SEE THE BANANA PEEL THAT THE MONKEY DROPPED!

4 LET THE PICTURES TELL THE STORY

In a comic, you can often read the story even if you don't know all the words. Encourage young readers to tell you what's happening based on the facial expressions and body language.

5 GET OUT THE CRAYONS

Kids see the hand of the author in a comic and it makes them want to tell their own stories. Encourage them to talk, write and draw!

Get kids talking, and you'll be surprised at how perceptive they are about pictures.

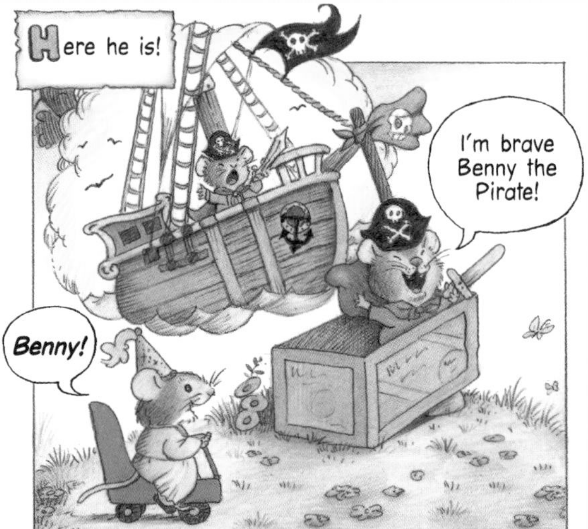
Here he is!
I'm brave Benny the Pirate!
Benny!

6 LET THEM GUESS

Comics provide a large amount of context for the words, so let young readers make informed guesses, and don't over-correct. In this panel, the artist shows a pirate ship, two pirate hats, and two pirate flags the first time the word "PIRATE" is introduced.